Study for
Obedience

Also by Sarah Bernstein

The Coming Bad Days

Study for Obedience

Sarah Bernstein

Alfred A. Knopf Canada

PUBLISHED BY ALFRED A. KNOPF CANADA

Copyright © 2023 Sarah Bernstein

www.penguinrandomhouse.ca

Knopf Canada and colophon are registered trademarks.

Epigraph on page vii by Ingeborg Bachmann from *Malina*, translated by Philip Boehm, published by Penguin Books, London, in 2019; epigraph on page vii by Paula Rego from an exhibition of her work (https://www.theguardian.com/artanddesign/2004/jul/17/art.art).

Library and Archives Canada Cataloguing in Publication

Title: Study for obedience : a novel / Sarah Bernstein.
Names: Bernstein, Sarah (Literature teacher), author.
Identifiers: Canadiana (print) 20230168965 | Canadiana (ebook) 2023016904X | ISBN 9781039009066 (hardcover) | ISBN 9781039009073 (EPUB)
Classification: LCC PS8603.E7622 S78 2023 | DDC C813/.6—dc23

Jacket image: 'Tapuit', 2004, Henk Helmantel
Photo: Art Revisited, Tolbert NL
Jacket design by Anna Green

Printed in Canada

10 9 8 7 6 5 4

Penguin
Random House
KNOPF CANADA

*For my pops, Nat Bernstein, who taught
me to love the sound of the words.*

1940–2022

'I can turn the tables and do as I want. I can make women stronger. I can make them obedient and murderous at the same time.'

PAULA REGO

'Language is punishment. It must encompass all things and in it all things must again transpire according to guilt and the degree of guilt.'

INGEBORG BACHMANN

Contents

1

A BEGINNING A BEGINNING AGAIN

It was the year the sow eradicated her piglets. It was a swift and menacing time. One of the local dogs was having a phantom pregnancy. Things were leaving one place and showing up in another. It was springtime when I arrived in the country, an east wind blowing, an uncanny wind as it turned out. Certain things began to arise. The pigs came later though not much, and even if I had only recently arrived, had no livestock-caretaking responsibilities, had only been in to look, safely on one side of the electric fence, I knew they were right to hold me responsible. But all that as I said came later.

Where to begin. I can it is true shed light on my actions only, and even then it is a weak and intermittent one. I was the youngest child, the youngest of many – more than I care to remember – whom I tended from my earliest infancy, before, indeed, I had the power of speech myself and although my motor skills were by then scarcely developed, these, my many siblings, were put in my charge. I attended to their every desire, smoothed away the slightest discomfort with perfect obedience, with the highest degree of devotion, so that over time their desires became mine, so that I came to anticipate wants not yet articulated, perhaps not even yet imagined, providing my siblings with the greatest possible succour, filling them up only so they could demand more, always more, demands to which I acceded with alacrity and discreet haste, ministering the complex curative draughts prescribed to them by various doctors, serving their meals and snacks, their cigarettes and aperitifs, their nightcaps and bedside glasses of milk. Of our parents I will say nothing, not yet, no. I continued to spend the long years since childhood cultivating solitude, pursuing silence to its ever-receding horizon, a pursuit that demanded a particular quality of attention, a self-forgetfulness on my part that would enable me to bring to bear the most painstaking, the most careful consideration to the other, to treat the other as the worthiest object of contemplation. In this process, I would become reduced, diminished, ultimately I would become clarified, even cease to exist. I would be good. I would be all that had ever been asked of me.

Better perhaps to begin again.

There was the house, standing at the end of a long dirt track and in a stand of trees, on a hill above a small, sparsely inhabited town. A creek marked the property boundary to one side, and at night the sound of its fretful flow came through my bedroom window. Looking down the long drive, one could see dense forest, a small town deep in the valley, and beyond, the mountains, higher than any I had seen before. The plot of land and the house which sat upon it belonged to my brother, my eldest brother. Why he ended up in this remote northern country, the country, it transpired, of our family's ancestors, an obscure though reviled people who had been dogged across borders and put into pits, had doubtless to do, at least in part, with his sense of history, oriented as it was towards progress, turned towards the future, ever in search of efficiencies. From a practical point of view – and pragmatism was naturally of the utmost importance to my brother – he was also engaged in some perfectly reasonable, if slightly perverse, business dealings, for he was, or at least had been, a businessman involved in the successful selling and trading, importing and exporting, of a variety of goods and services, the specifics of which to this day remain a mystery to me.

I came to stay in the house upon his request and initially for a period of six months, leaving the country of our birth for this cold and faraway place where my brother had made his life, had at any rate made his money, of which there was, as I would come to see with my very own eyes, a great deal. I saw no reason to object – I had always wanted to live in the countryside, had often driven through the rural areas surrounding my natal city in the autumn to see the leaves in colour, to experience the fresh air, so different from the turgid air downtown, well known to be the primary cause of the high rates of infant mortality, not that I had children myself, no, no, nevertheless, the air quality and its deleterious effects on public health were of concern to me as much as they might have been to any other ordinary citizen. Moreover, as my brother pointed out, it was not as though I had any specific obligations or ties that could not be broken with ease. I allowed this. Here is how it was. I had so to speak thrown in the towel. My contemporaries had long surpassed me, had, whether by treachery or superior skill, secured their places in life and in their chosen professions. It was said that it was a terrible thing to realise a lifelong dream, and yet still I wondered why they could not let blood a bit. They bloated with success. There was so much time and nothing to be done. I had only a little bit of will. I was not in on the great joke. For a time I pursued a career as a journalist but eventually left the news agency at which I had been employed, not even in disgrace, my time there had run its course, there was nothing at all to mark my going. My efforts over the years to obtain a continuous contract of employment had been in vain, the process had been explained to me as a bureaucratic and not at all a personal one, and yet when I responded in kind, that is to say by invoking the usual bureaucratic processes and fully within my rights making a request according to the general data protection regulation guidelines under the suspicion something fishy was going on, the application was treated as a personal affront and it was made clear to me that I was not helping myself. In truth, I never had helped myself. I left quietly. No one was sorry to see me go. The job I held just prior to my departure to my brother's home, in the country of our forebears, and which I would continue remotely from the same was as an audio typist for a legal firm, a job at which I excelled, typing quickly and accurately, knowing my work. Nevertheless, I sensed I was unwelcome in the office, which was lined with the usual legal appurtenances, binders and diplomas, leather and wood. I knew that my halting displays of personhood, my miserable insistence on continuing to appear in the office day after day, could only be disheartening to the jurists and paralegals whose voices I typed into a word processor swiftly, precisely, with devotion and even with love, and so they received my leaving announcement with unconcealed joy, throwing a farewell party in my honour, staging a kind of feast and donating lavish gifts. It did not take long for me to set my affairs in order, a matter of weeks, three months at the outside, and, the journey having passed without incident, here I was. The country air would be good for me, I felt, and the seclusion, when my brother did not need me I might take advantage of the various woodland paths maintained by local voluntary groups. I would be quiet.

At the time of my arrival, my brother was not yet ailing. Truly he was in the very pink of health, the prime of his life; having recently freed himself from his wife and teenage children and their perennial demands, he was, he said, at last free to pursue his business ventures in peace. His investments had begun to pay off and, in the absence of his family, from whom he had, it transpired, long felt estranged, and since he spent a great deal of time away from his home, he found himself needing someone to look after the house, he told me one afternoon over the telephone. And who better than I, who from childhood had proven myself the most efficient, most doting manager of my siblings' household affairs? When I did not respond immediately, he assured me that the house, although storied and ancient, although once belonging to the distinguished leaders of the historic crusade against our forebears, nevertheless had all the modern conveniences. These he enumerated, as though he were the agent of some new, dubious hotel: high-speed Internet, a variety of on-demand streaming services, a soaking tub, a rainfall shower, a memory foam mattress, hand-woven linens, a convection oven, a six-slice toaster, an ice machine, and so on and so forth. As my brother's claims about the furnishings of his home proceeded by this logic of declension, it occurred to me as it had perhaps occurred to him that he knew very little about me and, what's more, that this concerned him, the idea that he no longer knew what might please me. For instance, as he said the word 'mattress', his voice became suddenly panicked, as if he feared he had made the most irremediable blunder, that this mention of the mattress would be unacceptable, perhaps even offensive, to me. I was troubled by this sign of discontinuity in my brother's total authority, it was clear to me that the business with his wife must have come as a blow to him, what little I knew of men suggested that they were constitutionally incapable of being alone, terrified of not being admired, and seemed to regard ageing and its effects as a personal failing. Yes, yes, I said. Of course I would come. Of course! I said, nearly shouting into the phone. When had I ever denied him, my eldest brother, or any of the succession of other siblings whose whereabouts were just then unknown to me, when had I ever denied any of them the smallest request? Of course I would come. Naturally, he said, recovering himself, he would arrange and pay for my journey, he would pick me up himself at the airport in his car, a new model he had only just acquired, and drive me back to the house. And he did do these things, he never reneged on promises or went back on his word, no matter how rashly given, no matter how intoxicated or coerced he had been at the moment of avowal, although it's true in any case he gave his word freely and often, to friends and strangers alike, to business partners as well as adversaries, as far as my brother was concerned a thing, once said, was as good as done and that was all there was to it. When I exited the automatic doors of the airport, the navigation of which had taken me some time since the sensors did not at first register my movement, however exaggerated, so I had to wait until another recently deplaned passenger passed through the doors himself to exit, my brother's car was already idling at the kerb. Through the window, he gestured to me to get in, and I did.

On the drive from the airport to his home, some two hours away, my brother admitted that his wife, in collusion with the children, had decamped to Lugano, where her people lived, without a word and so far as he could tell permanently and perhaps even in the dead of night. The match had been doomed from the start, my brother said as he drove through the rain, they had shared too much about themselves, knew too much about one another for mutual respect to be possible. What's more, he went on, at various times, in alternating turns, they had committed the most grievous sins against one another, culminating finally in each speaking aloud the terrible truth of the other's personality, truths they had long known about themselves and about one another, but about which they had come to a tacit agreement never to mention, never to discuss, never to give away the slightest hint that such knowledge existed. The wife, knowing the essential flaw in the husband's heart, must never speak of it; likewise, the awful and indisputable fact of the wife's character, this too must never be spoken by the husband. No, my brother said, not ever. Such was the basis of the marital relation. I opened the passenger-side window and the wet spring air blew in. I watched the passing landscape, the pale, incipient green of something left too long in the dark, I watched the sodden black branches as they passed, and then, yes, came the smell of spring. I felt a thrill run through me.

I recalled my own aborted attempts at intimacy, with men, with women, and all that I had ever come away with was a sense of my essential interchangeability. People touched me, when they touched me, with a series of predetermined gestures in no way adapted to me, to my consciousness or sensations, limited though these were, insensible though I surely was. I had been so attentive to the particularities of their flesh, a smattering of freckles at the temple, bumps rising on the forearm, had cultivated this attention over time, painstakingly, aware of my inclination, congenital, towards vacancy, and yet this practice of contemplation never got me very far. My partners led me through the door, doing things to me they had done to others, doing things to me they could have done to anyone, anybody at all, and to put it plainly I was sure that, in each of their minds, with their eyes closed, they were with someone entirely other, not me – the tender kiss on the hairline, the holding of the back of the head, the grasping of the wrist, none of it was directed at me, all of it was for someone else, from before, some beloved, lost long ago. No, I thought, there was nothing I could say to my brother, no advice I could offer or consolation I could provide on the subject. All that was required, I felt, was one's silence. Not to speak, not to say. That's all.

And the children, my brother said, they too had always taken the part of their mother, he could see that now; from birth if not before they had sworn him off, found him ridiculous or else pathetic, a poor father and a sorry excuse for a man. If he was being honest, he had, he said, long felt these things about himself, and observing that his wife and children felt alike and expressed these feelings with such vehemence and at times, he had to admit, eloquence (for they were after all a family of readers), he was almost comforted. Although it would perhaps come as a surprise to me, he said with a sidelong glance, since he had been the eldest child, the most treasured, he had suffered. Yes, from childhood onwards, through the teenage years, into adulthood and to this very day, he suffered, and although his suffering had never been suspected by friends or relatives, nor even for the most part by himself, he said, running one hand through his thick, wavy hair, still, he knew. He had suffered. It was his truth and he had to speak it, at whatever cost.

I sat in silence, recalibrating my approach to my brother, pondering his new-found self-awareness, it was clear to me he had, as it were, found himself, likely with the collusion of a psychiatric professional of some kind. His demands on me, previously involving the undertaking of specific tasks and labours, the fetching or taking away of various objects, had evolved to more subtle matters of the mind. I was well versed in this office, too; throughout my life, people frequently unburdened themselves to me, telling me their most harrowing stories, the most appalling secrets of their inner lives, the whole litany of crimes and violations they had committed against others, and they told it all on the slightest acquaintance, on some occasions within moments of meeting. I did not ask for these confessions, I did not welcome them, I merely sat in silence, receiving them from all sides. Inevitably and ere long the people who unfolded these revelations were overcome first with regret and subsequently by a swift and silent loathing of me, perfectly understandable in any situation, and especially in this case. They would come to hate me as they had always hated themselves, for possessing this knowledge, for receiving it in the first place, for not doing anything to stop them passing it on. The lifelong loathing they held in their hearts, lifting at last, would attach itself to me for no reason other than my proximity, a certain sympathetic aspect I had, an air perhaps of docility that encouraged them to make these unbearable confessions. I knew it all, what to expect, and yet never had managed to stop it, to prevent the coming disclosure. From a long way away, I could identify a certain disposition, a slight lean to the left or something in the shoulder, I saw the annihilating confession approaching, and it fixed me in place, rendered me speechless. My brother, I knew, could not help but follow this same trajectory; by the set of his jaw as he drove the car and continued to speak, I knew the process was already well under way, and yet, like the others, he too went on speaking, as if compelled, for the duration of the car ride. I listened in silence. We drove at last through a small township and then beyond it, to my brother's house at the top of the hill.

2

A PROBLEM OF INHERITANCE

We made our way up the long drive beneath the stand of pines. I could see a dip where the creek ran down and away into the valley. It was a cloudy day, drizzling, the air suggesting ice. Spring thaw, a spell of danger lasting always longer than predicted, a promise unfolding and covering itself over once more, in frost, in a sudden snowfall. One had always to tread so carefully at the turn of the season, to keep one's wits. Who knew what might happen, what one might be capable of? The house appeared suddenly, dark against the dark of the trees, a series of blank windows that reflected only the weather back to itself. One house is much like any other, I told myself, fumbling with the seat belt, feeling my brother observing me. There was nothing particularly watchful about the place, the trees swaying mutely, the summit blind, the windows blind, a place of blind corners. Beside it all ran the creek, never the same, holding no memory. Nothing to be afraid of here, I thought, nothing lying in wait. My brother stood beside the car as I retrieved my suitcase from the boot, so composed he was, holding himself in such a dignified posture. He gazed up at the house, the old manor house, he went on to explain, which had been sold off by the gentry after the wars of the preceding century for any number of the usual reasons – death duties, dissolute relatives, the rising cost of fuel, the difficulty of finding adequate help to dust the mouldings, which were prolific, to oil the many long banisters or wax the vast wooden floors. Latterly, my brother said, the house's ownership had passed through the hands of a series of provincial upstarts, each more insolent than the last. During his own tenure he had endeavoured to restore the stately spirit of the place. It looked in other words much as one might expect a faded small-town manor house to look; my brother was nothing if not conventional, he would not have wanted to stand out, nevertheless even I was impressed at how precisely he had achieved the intended aesthetic effect, as if there had been no rupture in the house's historical lineage, as though he were the natural inheritor of the house and its grounds, of its contents, of the social status and indeed bloodline these things suggested.

The bedroom assigned to me was in the east corner at the front of the house, with windows that looked out on two sides – one upon the creek, high and full from the recent thaw, the other upon the long drive that led down into the valley and from there into the town. My brother slept at the back of the house, in a dark room whose windows were shaded by trees. Each morning I was to wake him with his breakfast tray, I was to open the curtains to reveal the forest that was his by deed of law, I was to lay out his clothes. While he ate, I would run his bath and, while he bathed, I would sit by him and read aloud the daily news headlines, clockwise as they appeared on the front page of the local newspaper. My brother was a tall man, strong and fit at that time, with good eyesight and a high level of reading comprehension. But he liked nothing more than to be waited on, to be read to, tasks his wife and children had previously undertaken in a complicated rota designed by my brother that ensured whoever had begun reading to him the coverage on, say, the latest political scandal at the county seat would be able to continue their reading of this story as it unfolded, until either the coverage abated or the corruption was rooted out, whichever came first. My presence simplified things, since all the tasks previously divided between my brother's wife and children would be my responsibility alone – the cleaning, the cooking, the shopping, the laundering, the airing out, the closing down, the warming up, the cooling off, the chopping of wood, the cutting of grass, the uprooting of weeds and many other things besides. My brother dealt with the payment of bills and invoices. Such free time as I had, as for example on weekend afternoons (for my brother was not an unreasonable man) or on weeknights after he retired to his bedroom, I spent roaming the surrounding countryside.

I thought we were getting along quite nicely when, only a few days after my arrival, my brother announced his intention to leave for a while, to go away, the legal complications related to his business were multiplying, he said, his clients were important, he was needed near at hand. It was true that since I had arrived, my brother had appeared nervous, not quite terrified but certainly not far from it, I could feel the tension in his back as I soaped it in the morning, a certain stiffness of posture when I dressed him, for I did like to dress him. I was disappointed at this news, so soon after our reunion, but comforted myself with the notion that his sudden departure meant I could roam more freely and at leisure, observing the frog life, which was prolific that spring, spawning in ponds and roadside puddles. I liked to sit under a tree by the creek and watch the creatures make their froggy way to the stiller pockets of water, both they and I watching out for the insects, newly emerged from pupae. Frogs had been a fixture of our childhood summers, my eldest brother often sent me out on excursions to capture a certain number of them, which he put to undisclosed use, even once a snapping turtle, an endeavour for which I employed a pair of tongs and a packet of frankfurters, lying on my belly on the dock every day for a week before I caught the creature, by which time my brother had moved on to some new project. I never knew what he did with the amphibian life I brought to him, and I did not ask, merely watched him as, with a shudder of pleasurable disgust, he peered over the edge of the red pail I was in the habit of using. On one particularly hot day, he placed two of the captive frogs side by side on the edge of the lake – one, much larger, my brother supposed to be a female, for reasons he would not reveal; the other, he said, clearly a juvenile male. My brother watched the frogs closely, with an anticipation I did not understand, until at all once, the larger frog turned and swallowed her companion whole. A single flipper flailed in her mouth. She swallowed again, and was still. I knew I must not weep, I must not scream, I must not run, though I wanted to do these things, yes, and to retch until my skin turned inside out. I was, it must be said, a sensitive child. My brother observed me closely. I knew he, together with the rest of my siblings, once they were informed, and who had been engaged in similar hunting operations nearby, would hold me responsible for this act of cannibalism, and they did, using it as further evidence, presented to our parents, who were at that moment sunning themselves quietly on the dock, of my essentially barbarous nature that needed to be controlled. And they did. They gave me direction. They gave me purpose. I lived for them. I lived especially for my brother, the eldest, the most handsome, most beloved of all of the siblings, so much energy and hope had gone into his conception and rearing. A firstborn son! The family was overjoyed, the siblings that succeeded him as well as the parents, we were all delighted, yes, we marked our eldest brother's achievements with especial attention, were studiously ignorant of his failings in school, in extracurricular activities, in the social sphere, as far as we were concerned, he could do no wrong. He never had to ask for anything and yet he did, he was voracious. He grew to be a teenager, tall for our family and fair-haired, dark-eyed, eventually an adult, he allied himself with certain kinds of people, took part in group chats where compromising images were shared of unconsenting individuals, he was a man at last and he was beautiful. He took a particular interest in me, the youngest, so many siblings in between him and me, so many years, the rest of the family allowed him this indulgence although they had marked me as a lost cause from birth, weak of lung, allergic to most fruits, a scrawny and pale infant with wispy hair. Nothing took with me, not convincingly, I was vague and inattentive, trailing off in conversation and, hopeless though I was, still my eldest brother took it upon himself to remedy these failings in me. He took me under his wing. I became his pupil and his retainer and he made me understand the necessity of temperance and silence. I had made an essential error when organising my consciousness early on in life, my brother explained, and this was by entertaining the idea that it was reasonable for me to form my own judgements about the world, about the people in it. It was not an uncommon error, my brother went on, but it was a conviction particularly unwarranted and also deep-seated in my case. It would not be easy to remedy, no, it would be my life's work to reorient all my desires in the service of another, that was the most I should expect to achieve. Seemingly, my brother told me, I was a girl, would perhaps one day be a woman, and it was up to me to ascertain how to gain mastery over myself. The character of a sister, the character of the brother: one to serve, the other to study, relations of kinship being various of course only in theory, one came up hard and often against tradition, against history, against the fact of the matter. And so such arrangements could be found up and down the suburban streets of one's childhood, they were not uncommon, no, not surprising for a sister to grind the meat, not at all remarkable that the brother in turn should sit in silent contemplation of his books, rock quietly back and forth in prayer. Each morning I composed myself, as perhaps others all along the suburban streets composed themselves too, before the bedroom mirror and descended the stairs in the skin of a sister. I took the role seriously, intentionally, and in time and with practice it became me. Perhaps in time my brother too became scholarly, became saintly, anything was possible, who in the final analysis could read the heart of another, but in the event and little by little, he encouraged me to pull in my skirts, which must remain metaphorical since I only wore trousers as a child, and I determined to eradicate my pride and my will.

I tried to be good. I smiled as I did the bidding of others. I did my work and looked perfectly happy, tidy and unobjectionable, shining, shining the boot. Kneeling, crouching, toing and froing, standing too for hours at the foot of a bed, later sitting perhaps on the edge of a chair, ankles crossed, thighs apart, a look that should have been an offering. I did as I was asked, yes, but the outcome was too often unanticipated. Some problem in me people always felt but could not prove. What did I give? The sword for the sponge. Muscular where one would not expect it. And then a troubling streak just perceptible, perhaps, in the gaze. Since girlhood I held a great sense of injustice, I was always rooting for the underdog, it was a matter of principle. On the question of standing up for what I believed in however I was somewhat less certain, perhaps even weak-willed, what resistance I presented was negligible. The difference between me and anyone else was not that I wanted more to be good, it was not even that I was guiltier, no, it was something rather difficult to place, a surface placidity with which I moved through the days, plodding, plodding, what certain teachers had in my youth described as a kind of idiot impenetrability, who could blame them, the school systems were overburdened, understaffed, and to be frank there were prolonged periods during which I refused to speak a single word anywhere on the school grounds. It was not a pursuit of affliction so much as an inborn quality, a gravity pulling me low. I had learned over the course of my life that there was something unpleasant about this opaque kind of inwardness: at any rate the people among whom I was reared demanded legibility – if there was one thing they could not stand it was the obscure, they were not a people much interested in the pursuit of meaning. They liked constancy. Another way of putting this is that they had the soul of the lake, not of the river, and not of the sea.

At home our parents rarely spoke. They allowed no past, no precedent, they were of that generation. What they had was what they made. They were the depression into which we all pooled, the weight of their expectations shaping our experience of belonging. The rules and structure of feeling of our household were transmitted by osmosis, the family nexus embodied in the parents, the siblings, trailing lines of tension and responsibility. I learned to be watchful. I watched my mother, never idle and yet lethargic as an earthworm, her life outside the house unimaginable, and yet she spent much of her time away from us, giving back to the community, being useful. My father too was often away, a businessman of some kind, demonstrating in his work a spirit we never saw at home. I watched my siblings come of age, try in vain to choose a life for themselves, wander a while, feeling the pull, feeling their betrayal, returning finally to settle in sight and in safety. Nobody ever said anything about it. I came to understand what that silence asked of me.

So by and by I learned to speak in slow, declarative sentences. I limited myself to simple exposition or straightforward and open questions. I erred on the side of caution and as a result I developed a reputation for being pliable and easy to use. And it is true that when confronted with other people, those other people who tended always to be after the upper hand, my will to powerlessness was brought out, I tended to be deferential, basically meek, tugging at the proverbial forelock until all my hair fell out. This attitude presented its own set of problems – namely, that meekness brings out the sadist in people, the atavistic desire to bite at the heels of the runt of the litter. As one writer put it, it's not the meek who inherit the earth. The meek get kicked in the teeth.

One morning for instance I stood eating a bowl of cereal by the window. In my brother's garden a kite plucked out the intestines of a grey rabbit. The rabbit had been alive until as recently as a few seconds before, death had not come swiftly enough for this rabbit, it had struggled. I had always loved the countryside, the north, trees in snow, but I had to tell the truth not expected to find quite so much violent death. I knew I would have to assimilate this death, even in time come to welcome it. My mind turned often now to the ways human joy, my own pleasure, was subject to death, how various were the ways death threatened to take it away. Whenever a branch fell in the forest after a storm, whenever the wind blew smoke back down the chimney, whenever my arm twinged, I thought, by long years of habit, supposing that is death itself? I had my boots on, ready to go; I had long ago settled my affairs. Still the agony of this rabbit affected me profoundly, I found myself weeping, and yet I could not pull myself away from the window, at a certain point I even raised a pair of binoculars which had been sitting on the sill to my eyes to get a better look at the particulars of the scene. My allegiance became confused. Although on the one hand the rabbit was small, fluffy and at a disadvantage, having neither wings nor talons, and although the rabbit looked more familiar to me, who had kept mammals as pets throughout my life, more familiar and even, it seemed, capable of love, or at least of a kind of devotion I might be able to recognise, it was true, I reflected, that the kite had needs, needed to eat, needed perhaps to feed its partner or infant kites, waiting somewhere in a nest, crying out, their survival depending upon it. There was also the matter of the rabbit's prolific relations, rabbits of various stripes could be found darting in and out of the hedgerows at any given moment, while the kites, I felt, without of course being able to prove it, procreated at a much slower rate. In taking a side, I thought uneasily, perhaps I ought to take the long view, the survival of the species as a whole. That was my problem, I thought, I was always thinking at the level of the individual, in this case the rabbit, the grim scene unfolding before me in the garden as the kite pecked at the belly of the poor beast, initiating a gyration in the corpse or almost corpse of the rabbit, a kind of organy wobbling. Now what was that that reminded me of? A hanging, tremulous, a doorway and a tidy garden. What happened to one's past when one got beyond it? That solitary life, the shadows on the bedroom wall at dawn, waking suddenly to the sound of the window rattling against the catch as a small pair of gloved hands tried to prise it open. But that was not it. What was required to make a life was the disclosure of space. In my case, for various reasons, not a carving out, but instead a reorientation of myself: form as a gesture of the will. I would become legible, I would flatten and disperse, inhabit a composite 'I', refuse my own plane of perception. There. Swallow the anticipatory view of my

life and live according to the contingencies of the other.
Attention as devotion. Sometimes I could just see myself
reflected, whole, as if on the other side of a smooth glassy
expanse, as though from a very great distance, a watery
light behind the clouds in January. The will to remain
essentially intact, for the pane not to lift, for no fissure
to appear in its surface.

To return to the rabbit and the kite. Was it a matter of
personal feeling, or was it a structure of ethics that was
and evidently would remain beyond my grasp? How
to choose? In the mornings of those first few weeks at
my brother's house, I cherished the silence. I stood at
my bedroom window and watched the greens emerge,
the trees, the mountains. How to describe how I felt
then, pacing the floorboards in my bare feet, unable to
tear my eyes away from the world outside, unable to
leave the porch, and finding it impossible to stay still.
I experienced a physical pain as I watched the crooked
pines blow in the wind. And then each time I cycled to
the outskirts of the town, not yet confident enough to
breach its limits, I pictured without surprise the bike
skidding off the road and into the creek running below

it, or else a load of logs coming loose from a truck bed and impaling me or crushing me to death. Or then again, I imagined losing my balance on the rocks as I took one of my preferred walks along the hill path, the axe slipping as I split a log, lodging itself in my thigh. I pictured any number of violent incidents resulting in injury or else death, yes, an array of potential painful deaths, deaths it must be said I had courted in both action and imagination, in both thought and deed. In short, the state of extreme precarity to which I had been accustomed up to this point, the state of permanent although latent terror that had characterised my existence until then, prevented me from believing my current situation was anything other than provisional, and as my desire increased to stay in the place forever, to remain at the mercy of the weather on the edge of the forest, so did my conviction that something, yes, something would intervene, something terrible would happen. From my chair by the window, I experienced a sensation of vertigo, as though at any moment I would be pitched head first into the situation outside. Much might be said about one's misfortune, according to one philosopher, but not that it was undeserved. I understood vaguely that I must confine myself to what was possible, but what was to be done when everything was refused in advance? To what extent was I responsible? As the spring came into itself the sun did not rise for it had not set. I was caught in the machinery of certain manias and maladies, the engines of their compulsory performance urging me on. And so as I tramped daily through the woods, feeling for once in the world, I told myself over and over that I must remember this moment, here, now, a moment which could not last and would inevitably be followed by an unhappiness that would be commensurate with if not exceeding it in strength, and that I must therefore carry it with me, the knowledge that once, for a time, for a series of hours, even stretches of days, I had seen what happiness might look like, that would have to be enough.

In spite of this anticipation of my general undoing, I was committed to maintaining the delicate equilibrium life seemed to have attained. I kept up with my work for the legal firm, continuing the transcription of the audio notes of one of the firm's partners, presently engaged by a multinational oil and gas corporation to pursue every possible course of action against a certain individual, who happened also to be a member of the legal profession, and who had sought to prove, indeed had proven in law in certain countries though not his own, gross malfeasance on the part of the multinational's leaders that had resulted in the poisoning of a number of water courses, the destruction of ancient woodland, the decimation of at least two protected species of birds, the kidnapping of activists and the corruption of public officials, as well as tax fraud, racketeering, stock-market manipulation and other crimes besides. The firm for which I worked, in representing this multinational oil and gas corporation, had already succeeded in having the attorney in question disbarred in several states, provinces, unincorporated territories and crown dependencies; in some but not all places he could no longer practise law, the only profession he had ever dreamed of pursuing, he explained in a podcast interview from his home, where he was at present under house arrest. The law had been his one true passion, his chosen path to the pursuit of justice, and he believed the spirit of the law would prevail. He hoped at least, he said in an undertone, to have his ankle monitor removed in the coming days, as it had been causing an allergic reaction that was both painful to experience and unpleasant to look at.

The voices of the various experts in law, my now-distant colleagues, came through my headphones and appeared almost instantly on the laptop's word processor. I was barely conscious of the act of typing, still less of the various processes of transcription going on inside me that turned the sounds into letters and the letters into words and then translated these words into movements in space on the part of my fingertips, which ticked away at the keyboard. I was at my best when I felt like a pure vehicle, a simple mechanism for the translation of sound into text, organised neatly into paragraphs, to be dated and signed. I typed and typed, trying not to listen too closely, balancing my attention on the fine point of understanding. If I could keep this balance, heeding the structure of what was said rather than parsing its significance, I could just about compose myself. The act of rendering another's words in this way evacuated the requirement for listening, the attention necessary was to the words themselves rather than to their meaning. It had been suggested at a certain point that I would be better off the less I knew about the matter and so I strove to understand as little as possible, even nothing, of what was said by my colleagues involved in the case. Word and word and word and word, they appeared on the page one after the other, accumulating fidelities, revealing sequence, producing clarity. It might be said that the lack of interest I showed in the substance of my work represented a failure of imagination, even an act of cowardice. It's true, I thought, pausing the audio, that imagination may be a moral faculty, as some writers have maintained, but how to understand its workings? What sort of self could be said to have an imagination? And was the self in this equation fixed, or was she mobile? If imagination was to be understood primarily in terms of morality, I needed to know how to cultivate it, I needed to understand the terms and structures of goodness and its pursuit. I never dared ask any of these questions aloud, merely took them into myself for the purpose of contemplation. The concept of cowardice was neither here nor there, I felt, but the charge of a lack of imagination was one I took seriously. Had I not spent my life imagining myself in the shoes of the other? Had I not done my utmost to see everything from other people's perspectives, rather than my own? The problem, I felt, was that I had, at a certain point, without noticing it, departed from the basic principle of my own wrong-doing on which my practice of doing good ought to have been based. The work of family, the domestic order. A problem. I went back to the beginning, starting the process again. Over and over. It was my practice and I repeated it often, particularly at such times as there was no one to remind me of that crucial and fundamental thing, the void at the centre of the work.

But here I find myself wandering again, into the past, which after all is not an explanation for anything, the lines of flight being so various, the question of harm and its reproduction so unanswerable, the beginnings always beginning again. This is a story about my brother, and so let us begin once more.

Prone as I was to idleness, I tried to keep to a routine in my brother's absence. Each day I unhooked the axe from its place by the back door and set to work splitting logs, one of my most important daily tasks for, while my brother had the most efficient central-heating system installed, although he had the house insulated to the rafters with the most modern technologies and at the greatest possible cost, and even though the rooms of the house reached more often than not blazing temperatures since my brother kept the windows closed and locked at all times, still he required the ambience and sense of history that only a log fire could provide. And so as I wielded the axe in my brother's name, and as I watched the bare branches toss against the sky, a feeling came over me, or else I felt surrounded by a way of feeling that preceded me and would carry on once I was gone, an awareness of catastrophe just beyond the garden gate, some small and precipitate decision of my own sending me careering towards it. After all, there was nowhere else to go, everything reached its terminus. It was an anticipation congenital, intermittent and providential. It was barely concealed and not totally unwanted.

All this was perhaps a problem of inheritance, I thought, the lullabies of my people, of my brother's people, of my and my brother's people, singing of

burning villages, of exile, in short, of a certain expectation of life passed on to us in babyhood. My people: for
yes, they were that, I had to admit it, after years of denial,
of immersing myself among strangers, if I had learned
anything it was that I had no people if not them, and yet
over the course of my adult life, and although I searched
high and low, there never seemed to be any around. I
occasionally looked up my schoolmates on the Internet,
their social media accounts full of photographs of large
suburban homes, identical in all respects to the ones in
which they had been reared. I remembered these houses
from childhood – the bare, shining floorboards and per-
petual aroma of clean laundry rising from the basement,
the space and privacy afforded even to the youngest
offspring. I adored these houses, I envied the odious
children and the frictionless way they moved through
the world, they gave the impression of being clean and
without history, like gentiles, like people unstained by
ancestral shame. I learned early on that money could
clean you up and make you anybody. My brother, I felt,
had learned this, too, purifying himself, moving through
the world with fluency, the only thing he allowed to

shape his destiny was his will to accumulate and wield power in the world, in all its various spheres. The past, as far as I could tell, was not holding any of them back. For my part I learned that nobody got what they deserved. In the intervening years, as I scrolled or clicked through these photographs, I often wondered which of us could be said to be more perverse: my schoolmates, every last one of whom, it appeared, had turned away from the world, retired to their enclaves, chosen the lives of their parents; or I, who had been plagued since childhood with the feeling that I needed to scrub myself clean, that all that was needed to be free was to physically remove myself from the company of people who comprised the community in which I had grown up, as though life were easy, or even possible.

I had been a disappointment in so many ways, I often reflected, to my parents and siblings, who could not understand my perversity in this or any other regard, to my extended family, for much the same reasons, and to my teachers, in whose presence I steadfastly refused to say the bracha over our classroom Sabbath ceremonies each Friday afternoon. It was the one act of defiance I allowed myself in childhood, and it came to define me, no matter how hard I worked to be good, so long as I persisted in this unaccountable refusal to join in, the light of grace was and would continue to be withheld from me. In later years, it was enough for my intransigence to be suspected, no matter how stilled my lips, how low my head, no matter how I allowed myself to be used for the benefit of others, still goodness eluded me. As to my friends, I had none, although at school I had been briefly popular when it was revealed that the great-nephew of a famed writer of Holocaust memoir had held my hand. My proximity to this boy, a sort of community celebrity, made me acceptable, even slightly desirable, briefly, all too briefly. Our liaison did not last long, as the boy soon discovered my predilection for self-flagellation which, though not necessarily a tendency that was in itself uncharacteristic of our people, I had inflected with a strange and unwholesome character, he told me, not in so many words. I had lost much in the intervening years, and what I had learned was that it was no bad thing to stay in place. At last, I felt, I had arrived, in this place where our ancestors were born and whence they had fled, where my brother had chosen to live, where I had no right to a passport or citizenship documents of any kind though my brother had managed to procure these and more, much more, for himself.

And so, when my brother departed, just a few short days after my arrival, he left me to look after the house and also his dog, whose existence I had only just discovered, a small and sickly animal that spent its days, so far as I could tell, retching what little food it managed to choke down back up again on to the rugs and carpets of my brother's home. It was difficult to discern the breed of this dog, so matted was its fur, so crabbed its limbs, of which as far as I could tell there were only three, and so unusual the sound it made, but it was a sort of light brown colour, and my brother called it Bert, he said, introducing the creature into my arms. The dog as it happened had some problems with his testicles, the veterinarian had recommended castration, an outcome my brother could not accept and said so, in no uncertain terms, but the veterinarian insisted, an argument ensued, the authorities were involved, and finally my brother had been compelled to give the veterinarian

43

leave to remove the dog's testicles, he explained, pointing at the raised pink scar near the dog's privates. One could scarcely laugh at my brother. When he spoke, his words seemed to take on an actual presence in the room; they appeared credible, even demanded an anxious kind of respect. I nodded seriously in response. He looked away from me, disgusted, before rolling his carry-on bag across the floor of the entrance hall and out the door.

It took several days and a number of encounters with his few remaining fangs, but at last the little dog Bert and I got to know one another, arriving at a mutual if hesitant respect. I kept to my routine, going for walks through the woods and up on to the moor; given his various physical ailments, Bert did not accompany me on these perambulations, wisely limiting himself to a slow and deliberate description of the terrace to one side of my brother's house. But Bert and I spent quite a few lovely afternoons together on this terrace, or in the garden beyond, which was lined with laurel hedging, I sunning in a chair, he sniffing the perimeter, we keeping our distance from one another but nevertheless getting along pleasantly. I had never particularly liked dogs

nor had they ever taken to me, but Bert was a thought-
ful creature, a ratcatcher, with an air of quiet dignity
about him arising perhaps, I thought, from his physical
malformations.

In the days and weeks that followed my brother's
departure, something in me quietened. It was as if I
had been living my life against the backdrop of a roaring noise that I had not known was there and that had
ceased suddenly and absolutely. My perceptions turned
outward. I saw the grass grow, I saw it growing, I saw
the green changing, noticed the new heights reached
by the branches. I paid such close attention. It was dis-
orienting to walk in the woods day after day, to mark
the astonishing and impossible changes from one day
to the next. I was dizzy with it all. I felt as though I were
remembering something I had long forgotten. For one
thing, there was the wind. For another, the silence,
which seemed to open out and across my surroundings
the longer I stayed in the place. My habitual walk was up
the wooded hill behind the house, crossing a series of
low and boggy places as well as higher and harder well-
drained ground. I walked these woods daily, attending

one day to the treetops, on another to the branches, or else to the minute plants at the bases of the trees, the mosses changing colour. In spite of this close attention, it remained for me a landscape that had no names: the plants were different from the ones in the country I had left, which anyhow I would not have been able to identify, and my Internet searches could bring up no English results. Since I could not interpret the diacritic marks of the language of the country, the shape of the words in my mouth could only be an approximate homophonic translation. And so although I walked in the forest nearly every day of the year, I felt perpetually estranged from it, as indeed I had felt estranged from most of the settings in which I had found myself over the course of my life.

About four miles behind the house, up beyond the treeline, in a dip between some hills, there was a small freshwater lake. A thin layer of ice still covered the surface of the water when I arrived that spring, and I liked to lie on my front at the water's edge and watch the strange shapes moving beneath me. The spot was relatively protected and after the sound of the wind in the pines, the silence rang and rang. As I returned to this lake over the months that followed, I learned that this quality was intrinsic to the place: it was not merely the contrast of the wind and the stillness; the thrum of silence at the lake exerted a physical pressure that, while not painful exactly, overwhelmed me, pinning me to the spot, often for hours at a time. At times the silence was a sound: a humming, like a refrigerator in an empty house at night, it was tangible, I felt it as much as I heard it, and yet I knew that what I felt and heard was a nothing, something that was not there. There were no trees for the wind to blow through, no electrical wires either above or below the ground, only the ground itself, covered, that first time I visited, in frost. And yet there it was: presence and absence twisting together. Over the course of my life, so much of which I had spent in solitude, I developed a habit of speaking aloud, to myself or to my surroundings: at times this was to offer encouragement, some kind word to help me carry on, in spite of it all; at others to offer observations on the passage of time. In the bowl of the lake, my voice came back to me, and it sounded closely – it was more intimate than ever. I spoke and listened to myself at length as I watched the dark shapes move under the thinning ice. I cannot say whether I was ever overheard while I occupied myself in this way: if I had been, it would have been only one behaviour among many others, truthfully or falsely reported, that would later be held against me.

3

A DYING TONGUE

What needs explaining was that, and it was a funny thing, a very funny thing, I did not speak the language. It was not for lack of trying, for I had been enrolled in a programme of daily language tuition for six weeks prior to my relocation, tuition I continued remotely upon my arrival in the place. I was studious. I was meticulous. For whatever reason it would not stick. I had never had a problem with language acquisition up to that point, from childhood I had spoken four languages, at least two of which I had lost in the passage of time, all the same I pursued in a haphazard manner my studies of foreign languages at university, picking up German and Italian with ease, in fact the facility with which I read and wrote, not to mention conversed, in these languages after barely a month's attendance at weekly classes floored my instructors of German and Italian, in no small part because of a certain vacant quality I had always had. The teachers lavished me with praise, holding me up as an example in front of my classmates, who despised me with good reason, in the first place because I appeared to relish the attention, taking every opportunity to answer the questions the teachers posed to us, delivering sentences with multiple clauses to showcase my linguistic virtuosity, revelling in every single syllable as it rolled off my tongue and into the space of the classroom in which I sat, together with my classmates, who observed the spectacle with silent loathing, suspecting I had prior knowledge of the languages and was in point of fact a cheat. But the mother tongue of the locals foiled me, as it did not foil my brother, who had long mastered the language, who even as a child loathed any sign of weakness, who always sided with the victors, whatever their stripe. For a long time it did not occur to me that my brother had come to the town for just this reason, not an overwriting of history so much as a realignment of himself with the powerful, the crowning achievement in a lifelong pursuit of dominance.

But here again we go too far. Let us confine ourselves to our own motives. With regard to the problem of language, it was not the weather of the place that hindered me, for I liked the cold, had been born in the wintertime, as a child had often lain down in the snow, in my snow-suit, and looked up at the white sky for hours, for hours. The situation in this northern country town seemed to me to offer a robust life, a hale life, a life of people with smooth and youthful skin, a much healthier lifestyle, in short, than I had been accustomed to, and my brother, prior to his illness, had been exactly this sort of vigorous person, could be found, at any given time, running a marathon or energetically and in a team rowing a skiff on rough seas. I on the other hand had been a dedicated and lifelong smoker, I loved nothing more than a smoke, it's true, from the age of fourteen I could be found smoking on street corners and doorsteps, in alleyways and in stairwells, and yet I was a stationary smoker, never moved while smoking, hated the sensation of smoking while walking, and I walked plenty – if I had a second, not quite equal, love, it was walking, I spent entire days walking from one end of the city I lived in to the other and back again, travelling by foot from tram terminus to tram terminus, bus station to bus station, municipal park to industrial park, and back again, always back again. I felt these were pleasures that ought not to be mixed, I had always wanted to be good and so, as a kind of offering of gratitude for my new life, I gave up smoking, which was just as well, for I had enough to be getting on with, as it turned out.

At first I stayed away from the town in the valley, supplementing my brother's stores of dry goods with vegetables from the overgrown kitchen garden. I got to know my immediate surroundings. I walked around the house, inside and out. I stood under the pines on the long drive, under the stand of alders by the creek, by the birch trees at the edge of the forest. I felt the cold ground of the kitchen garden give beneath me as I knelt down, so many hours spent weeding, mending the fences and darning the netting that cradled the winter crops. I untangled the tender leafy greens from the viny plants that had grown around them, wondering about the lives of cabbages, their hearts and their vitality. They did not know, how could they, the care and attention with which I applied myself to them, and I loved them for that, the essential mystery of their being, no exposition possible, no question of knowing or being known, the beautiful, the unthinkable cabbages! The kales too, and the mustard greens, even the garlic, having survived the winter, throwing out its slender stalks. Do you understand what I am saying? Beauty is something to be eaten: it is a food. I endeavoured to learn from staying in place. I studied under the plants, under the earthworms, I felt the texture of the earth in which all these organisms lived changing with the seasons. How, I wondered, might a person, a people, take root? Roots and rootlessness, the preservation of what little remains of the past, such were the thoughts that blew through me on any given morning, standing very still in the porch, or in the garden in my bare feet, feeling suddenly: that sound, that rushing, it is the wind, it is the trees! Once, during a storm, a willow, too shallowly rooted, had come down. I went to look at it the following morning, under a still and clear sky. It was a young tree with long red osiers – now why should that have made me so terribly sad? I stood by it for a while before, and this is unaccountable, reaching down and clipping off its branches with some shears I kept in the pocket of my dungarees. What could I possibly have wanted with those switches of willow? It was as if I was animated by some external force that directed my actions, I found myself putting them away to dry, picking them up again one or two weeks later, weaving them into baskets, some current in my body guiding my hands, which up to that point had displayed no aptitude for crafts, no, not even the most basic motor skills, I had always been blundering, and yet still I found the basket taking shape before my eyes. Was it possible for muscle memory to be historical? The patterning of the basket, this particular basket, passed down through the generations, living in latency, only just activated in me, inexplicably, on a clear day after a storm. On another morning I found myself clipping reeds, weaving these into various shapes and figures, which I lined up along one of my bedroom windows. What were they for? Company, yes, external signs of my existence, of my living self. And then also gestures of thanksgiving to the place, offerings to the world around me.

Sitting one afternoon on a rock by the creek, I observed the water running under the melting ice, carving out patterns, and then the ice itself, in its incalculable shades of white and grey and blue, how long and lovely and terrible the springtime, how unbelievable to be alive. If I could be anything, I thought, sitting on my rock, eating a granola bar, I would be that ice, with its multitudes, always in the process of transformation. It was not long before I took to immersing myself, of course I did, in the lake on the hill, breaking up the clear layers of ice with my walking stick, treading slowly into its dark waters, deeper and deeper, feeling on the brink of something, of sinking, I thought, not knowing what else to call it. Another way of putting this is I began to take note of the rhythms of the place, and even, from a distance, of the town.

There was, for instance, the strange behaviour of the dogs. Three times a day, at daybreak, at noon, at sunset, in all corners of the township however far-flung, every canine, as if mobilised by some mysterious force, stood to attention and howled in one long, unbroken, collective howl. And there were other peculiar occurrences, some more alarming than others, but I will get to them in time. The people, for their part, so far as I could tell, had closed, white faces. They had I am sure characters of their own, interests of their own, but such things were difficult to discern from a distance. Nevertheless, I continued to observe them just as they, I know, observed me. Patterns became apparent, days of work and rest, feast days, market days, days set aside for religious devotion. I began to love the town in the valley, which seemed, from my vantage point in my brother's house on the hill, so tidy, so well ordered. I began to love the people, whose history I knew was so entwined with mine, whose ancestors had lived side by side with mine, had worked with them, broken bread with them, lived under the same sky, suffered the same cold, the same blight, the same floods, the same kinds of catastrophes, for a time, for a time. For all things come to an end, yes, as the lives of my forebears had come to an end, life itself and life as they knew it, never knowing, never understanding why or wherefore, only that a feeling, running under the seams for centuries, had broken to the surface. How then could I not love these people, who represented the closest thing to an inheritance I could be said to have? I wondered how they would receive me. Of course I had heard stories of other such meetings, of spitting and stones, of defacements and assaults, but these people, I felt, were different, they were serious, devout. Above all, I sensed, they understood the importance of perceiving things without using their names, that names were secret, they were sacred.

The time eventually came when I was required to leave the seclusion of the house and the woods and go into town for provisions. I knew that, whether or not I intended it, I would be presenting myself in public as the representative of my brother, as the one person, absent his wife and children, looking after his affairs. I could show no sign of weakness. I would do him proud. I dressed with care in one of the many loose linen garments I had acquired over the years and a long coat against the weather and set out on foot along the road, a single paved track that led down into the valley, where at a certain point it intersected the few subsidiary streets that comprised the town. At the centre of the town there was a church, there was nothing sinister in that, and around the church, a churchyard. I had always had a feeling for churches, especially country churches such as this one, surrounded by trees, planted perhaps at the time of the church's construction, the church and trees growing together over the years, over the centuries, such a long and unbroken life this town had! I imagined the scrubbed wood benches, the kneeling on flagstones, the spareness of it all, I admired churches greatly, yes, and yet I confess I had never set foot in one, had then as now a superstitious fear of crossing the threshold, passing up the chance to see inside some of the world's most famous churches and cathedrals on tours in my youth. But still, I liked to look out the window of my room on the second floor of my brother's house, down into the valley, and see the church spire rising out of the trees, it felt like, as indeed it was, a meeting point – of life, of the spirit – some kind of organising principle I had tried in vain my whole life long to live up to. There was so much one had to live up to, so many good deeds one had no reasonable expectation of carrying out, because of one's resources, because of one's will, and they would loom over the whole of one's life, these specific failures, representing metonymically as it were the profound spiritual failure of one's life, the community always holding one to account. In the Church it was different. In the Church, I felt, one began from the principle of original sin, one's guilt assumed from the get-go. From childhood I felt always on some precipice, reaching for a state of grace, ever unattainable to me, always on the point of falling. I tried yoga, I tried harmonising with Mother Earth, but only scraps of it took with me. I liked looking at the church spire perhaps because I saw in it the possibility of a life of obedience where one's sins had been acknowledged and already redeemed. Such were my thoughts as I walked into town that first time, crossing the road to get a closer look at the crocuses emerging in the churchyard, smiling up at the church itself, still there after all these years, never succumbing to fire or flood, to natural disaster or man-made catastrophe, a place whose doors were kept immemorially unlocked, a place where confidence gathered, bringing the people along with it. In truth and as it happened a building further away from God one could scarcely imagine.

Driving the town's economy, my brother had given me to understand, was, or at least had been, a trade in tombstones, in which he himself naturally had a hand. The quarries still brought up stone for this purpose, a dwindling number of carvers still carved it, and the finished stones were sent to mark the resting places of the dead all across the country. Much of the land in the township was owned by this quarrying company, but there remained a small community-run farm for the growing of fruit and vegetables and the rearing of livestock, such as cattle and sheep. Perhaps, my brother had said over the phone one evening, I might find some small, harmless way to become involved in the endeavour, make an effort to assimilate into the local community, take part for once in the things happening around me. There was a rota sheet in the shop, he explained, where one could sign up for such tasks as milking, feeding, walking, shearing, grading, carding, spinning, lambing, cleaning, digging, weeding, strimming, mowing, tilling, sowing, seeding, walling, liming, scraping, watering, erecting, dismantling, soldering, separating, hitching, unhitching, mucking out and transporting to slaughter. My brother had not specified which of the aforementioned I might be qualified to undertake, nor did he provide any advice with regard to the particulars of how to go about communicating my intention, my difficulty in learning the common speech was still painful to him, he was ashamed and even offended, owing it to some wilfulness on my part.

The single track that ran from my brother's house became, down in the valley, the town's main street, where one could find the shop, a kind of general goods store. It stood on a paved lot, empty but for a lone petrol pump, a low wooden building lined with windows, over the entrance of which hung a neon sign in cursive script giving the name of the place. Underneath this was a second sign, striped yellow and white, that read: Café. For, I noticed, peering through a window, one half of the space had indeed been given over to a number of booths, to a counter with a row of stools, where people sat eating such fare as one might expect to see in a roadside diner of this kind, admitting of course certain regional variations, such as the type of berry used in the pie, the thickness of the chips, the kind of toast served alongside the plate of eggs, the brand of cherry cola, and so on and so forth. The far-reaching and long-lasting influence of mid-century American road culture might be cited here, though it hardly needs explaining at this point in history, cultural imperialism, military imperialism, the long march of the American diner, its rise and fall, its rise again in the present age of nostalgia, when one finds oneself yearning for a landline, for a rotary dial, for the hard edges of a VHS cassette, for the smell of the video store on a Friday night, for the commercial life of another era when one knew slightly less, for one's personal golden age, yes, yes. From the outside, the shop, and especially the diner appeared like a haven from the age of anxiety, not to say terror, in which one lived. I wanted so badly to be able to sit alone in one of the booths and drink a cup of coffee that would be refilled periodically by a server, smoke a cigarette perhaps, have a slice of pie. It would be a long time, I reflected, before I could gather the courage to sit in the diner on my own, I would first have to brave the aisles of the shop, the counter where, no doubt, the shopkeeper presided over her till.

That first time I entered the shop I was in an extreme state of agitation, I so wanted to make a good impression on the shopkeeper and yet knew there was no hope of my doing so, as a result of my continuing failure to learn her mother tongue, we could not communicate other than by pointing and nodding, and although it was common in the country for people to speak English, I could not count on anyone being willing to use it. Thus, the anticipated difficulty was twofold: first, in the failure more generally of my own expression which, when not plagued by aphasia – receptive or expressive – or dysphasia, of the same orders, when not affected by aphonia, by a stutter or a lisp, by the loss of control of my vocal cords and sometimes the muscles in my face, was, at the best of times, ambiguous and even obscure. Second was the problem of comprehension on the part of the listener, taking into account the language divide, the listener's incapacity or unwillingness, their degree of hearing loss – congenital, selective, injury-induced or as a natural result of ageing – and a number of factors besides. And so each time someone might try to speak to me, to place me, to find out where I came from, though they would already and without a doubt have the information second-hand from my brother who as I say spoke fluently, having mastered the regional accent and even the local idiom, his difference was barely perceptible, his proximity to the dominant culture within a hair's breadth, I felt a renewed sense of shame and failure for being unable to do the same, for providing further evidence of the arrogance of English speakers, the way they contrived, by virtue of their tongue, to bring destruction with them wherever they went in the world, and I was sorry for the townspeople who, I knew, must, with the passage of time, only grow to resent this failure. And so as I stood in silence before the counter in the town shop on that first visit, in a state of heightened confusion, attempting to count out the currency that was still unfamiliar to me, and doing so with what must have seemed to any onlooker like deliberate and obstructive slowness, I groped for something to rescue the situation.

My eyes alit on a piece of lined yellow paper where other
people had signed their names in hand-drawn boxes,
names I could not read. I knew, or at least felt, that this
must be the rota sheet for the community farm. My gaze
roved to the single empty space, and before I could stop
myself, I grasped the pen lying on the counter, a bolder
action than I was accustomed to taking, and wrote in my
name. As I did so, I told myself that it behoved me, after
all, to give up my free time to this community initiative,
to do something to show my gratitude for the beautiful
place in which I lived, for my life which had proceeded
up to that point without any major tragedy or disaster,
no serious injury, no debilitating illness, no poverty or
homelessness, no addiction or sudden psychological
break, no love lost having never been gained, no kidnapping or attempted murder, no extortion or blackmail, no
assault that had been reported, investigated and brought
to trial, no genocide or exile in my generation, I had been
fortunate, yes, luckier than most, I ought to do my part,
to serve the community, to pay what I owed. I replaced
the pen in its holder and ventured a look at the shopkeeper. Her mouth was in a thin, grim line and she had

one hand under the counter, reaching, I thought wildly, for a weapon of some kind, yes, I thought, my time had come, naturally, and I deserved it, for although on the one hand I felt I was expected to perform community service; on the other, I had come forward without first having been asked, without knowing the details of the project or the ways of doing things into which the townspeople had without a doubt been inculcated since infancy and which I would struggle to master despite all my best intentions and sincere efforts. I had always been awkward, even completely inept, and I realised with horror that in signing my name to this rota sheet, ostensibly to offer my assistance, I had in fact placed a burden on the townspeople to teach me how to do things, to explain by gesture and with difficulty their ways of being, the local practice of animal husbandry, to give up their own limited time only so that I could feel good about myself, about my participation in society. It would be no bad thing, I had long felt, for someone to put me out of my misery, at any rate it was too late to rectify my error, I could not now remove my name, not so soon and not under the watchful and suspicious eye of the shopkeeper. I stood for a moment, holding my breath, waiting for the shopkeeper to raise her hand from beneath the counter, which she did, and it was empty, and so, I reasoned, she must therefore have pressed some kind of security alarm hidden cunningly beneath the counter, to summon guards or the local police force, to release the large black dog I had seen kennelled behind the shop. I looked around, fully expecting to see a group of men, a group of women, a pack of dogs coming through the front door, through the door leading to the storeroom, but nothing happened, no one came. When my gaze fell once again upon the shopkeeper, she did not seem to be smiling, no, not quite, but she took the coins and bills from my hand and counted out what she felt was the correct amount for the items I had placed on the counter in what now seemed some distant past. She held the door open for me as I left, I had purchased more things than would fit into my tote, out of guilt, out of terror, and I was required to carry in my hands certain items like a punnet of strawberries grown in the town's polytunnel, a bottle of milk from one of the local goats, a box of eggs from the chickens. The shopkeeper did not chivvy me out, and yet the door closed swiftly behind me so that I found myself suddenly and once again in the car park, looking at the single fuel pump which, I noticed for the first time, was owned and supplied by the company the legal firm I worked for was currently representing. Lives layered upon lives, the concentric logic of the world and its continual co-optations. I felt a motiveless sorrow.

And yet, I thought, popping one of the strawberries in my mouth, it was spring. There was that. Of course, the gulls picked off the ducklings, the hooded crows the chicks, and the wild geese ruminated on the meagre ground. No grass grew, only daisies. The lean and hungry season endured, of course, of course. But still a few things grew, still there was life. Day after day I affirmed the silence, chewing, chewing the cud. In his home, my brother had a number of stone sculptures made by a local artisan. In his studio which overlooked one of the many creeks that ran through the area, this man carved images of the area's wildlife in stone from the local quarry. From the privacy of his home, he wrote numerous letters of complaint to the local authorities, who had in turn passed them on to my brother. My brother loved these notes, took great pleasure in them, how beautiful he found them, written in flowing script, meticulously paragraphed, full of demands and interludes on the soul. He would sleep no more, one letter began, my brother said. He would contact his lawyers and the lawyers of the relevant landowners. There would be, he wrote, in that exquisite hand I had never seen personally but could imagine so well in my mind's eye, no wind turbine; there would be no deer fencing, there would be no planting of trees or management of rushes, no bees, no new builds, no council tax on second homes or short-term lets, no tourist tax, no reintroduction of beavers, no wildcats, no bears, no foxes, no foreigners, only things as they had always been, only Nature and the gaze. O rhododendrons! (They grew in profusion around his house.) O such themes! I thought I had seen him once, walking in the road to town, which was overhung with trees still in the process of becoming. He had a head of thick white hair and wore a shirt, unbuttoned to mid-chest. He was deeply tanned. He walked with dignity.

Here, I thought, as I made my slow way home, my fingers stained by the new, fresh berries, here was what came to the surface after so many throes and convulsions. Soon we would no longer need to withdraw to the desert for a space of contemplation and self-abnegation. Soon, personal ascesis would arrive in the form of one more letter, one more mass mortality event, one more migration stopped by total annihilation. Nature and well-being, the Home Office, any number of crooks and lowlifes. I wanted to be good in the terrible world. I thought of the birds. I accumulated fidelities in this space of diminishing returns. On the one hand, I felt that my obedience had been rewarded at last. On the other, in this cold and beautiful countryside, I feared I was living a life which I had done nothing to earn and I felt sure of some swift and terrible retribution. As I bit into the last strawberry, I began to weep because language, I felt, was no longer at our disposal, because there was nothing in the word that we could use. Nothing settled in place.

I cannot now explain what impelled me to go into the forest that night, to pick the herbs and grasses I knew so well by sight though not by name, to weave them into shapes of some significance to me, and then to proceed on my bicycle, in the small hours of the morning, while the townspeople slept, while the moon traced its nocturnal course, to deliver these several talismans to select locations in the village. The farm, which seemed so central to the life of the community; the shop, likewise. I also made sure to bless the places I felt to be sacred to the sleeping townspeople with my offerings – their church, the town square where the weekly market took place – as well as the homes of those I knew to be dignitaries. Before each of these places I said some quiet words of devotion and, when I had made my rounds, got back on my bicycle and rode to my brother's house. On my return I slept deeply, a thick and dreamless sleep.

While I waited for the verdict of my application (for so I saw it now) to work in the town's smallholding, I could not settle. As a way of managing the empty time, I created a schedule for myself, planning my activities to the quarter hour, designing slots in which I might contain myself. I began to hook rugs, hideously, out of old sheets and other assorted rags that I backed with hessian sacking I found in my brother's attic. I gifted these to Bert, who urinated on them directly. I carried on foraging for flowers and herbs that looked more or less like those I researched in a book on medicinal plants, hoping to derive from them some healing essence. The reed men, which I continued to weave with such affection, still sat lined up on the sill in my bedroom. I had no particular objective in making these figures: their arrival on the doorsteps of certain townspeople had as yet generated no response. One never knew how one's gifts might be received. I walked often, for long distances, listening closely to my breathing, guiding it in and letting it out to counts of three, or four or five. I took circumscribed routes in an effort to minimise the chance of any unexpected or unwanted encounter. I dressed with care, according to the weather, from foot to head, beginning with the woollen socks whose seam I aligned precisely with the front of my toes; followed closely by the boots, lined or unlined depending on the season. From there I would pull on my underpants, over which went the walking trousers, got on with difficulty, yes, given the boots, already so tightly laced. The shirt followed the undershirt, over which, of course, the jumper. A jacket, perhaps, or a waterproof. Upon my pate, my hair, where it grew, and upon my hair, a hat. In this way I would ready myself for the walk, whether short or long, whether easy or arduous, I took all possible precautions with regard to my clothing. Following these preparations, I would take the walking stick from its place inside the front door and inch my way abroad in silence, not wanting to disturb the spirit of the house within and likewise not wanting to alert any living thing without to my presence. I crept along the path that led up behind the house, tiptoeing, holding my breath, until I reached a certain distance away and felt certain that I was not being observed, who after all would bother with me, I could hold no possible interest for anyone, I was merely going for a walk in sensible, weather-appropriate apparel, out of sight of the town or any other human habitation, having no intention of staying long in any particular place, certainly none of leaving a mark of my presence, were such a thing even possible, and yet since the submission of my name to the townspeople, I had felt – how else to describe it – some feeling or intent bending towards me. I had no knife with me, no matches, not even a compass to find my way should I lose myself in the forest or on the high moor. My clothes were made of natural fabric and, should they be discarded for any reason, would decompose in time, return to the earth, providing it with nutrients, encouraging new growth. Yes, I trusted in providence to guide me, and, as it happened, I never did get lost.

At the same time, and even on these clearly demarcated walks, I found much to disturb the sense of stability and containment I was working so hard to achieve. Gates locked where one previously had the right to roam. Paths one walked regularly now overgrown, barely traversable. I would return from these outings exhausted, as if the land itself, which previously had been completely indifferent to my presence, had noticed me at last, and unfavourably, and was working to expel me. If this was not quite the trajectory I had hoped for, it was nevertheless no more than I had any right to expect. Who was I? Why had I come? I was not from the town, that much was clear, not even from the surrounding areas, and, unlike my brother, I lacked the essential quality that would have enabled me to overcome these basic failings. I was not from the place, and so I was not anything. I was a nothing, a stranger who was not wanted but who nevertheless imposed herself continually, day after day, a kind of spectral presence hovering at the edges of the life of the town, whose intentions were obscure and who for some reason evinced a terrible fidelity to the idea of staying put. The spring landscape seemed to reinforce these impressions of mine, that there was no place that would remain undisturbed, no place I would find peace from the consequences of each misstep, pathetic or deliberate, I had made since arriving. Such was the course of my thoughts when I returned from my walks, the lines along which I could be found thinking as I undressed myself in reverse, from top to toe, removing the hat from the hair on the pate, the jacket from the jumper, the jumper from the shirt, the shirt from the undershirt; moving thence to the trousers, pulled once more but in the opposite direction over the boots, removing the underpants in the same manner, unlacing the boots, slipping off, finally, the socks and placing my feet on the hardwood floor. The procedure completed, I would sit on the bed for a moment, practising mindfulness, using my breath to calm my body and my spirit, slowing down the thoughts until gradually, very gradually, nothing remained. Yes. Then could I see clearly. As for being easy in my mind, I could never be that, no, but that, I felt, was my salvation.

Once, I came across a pregnant ewe who had become tangled in a section of dilapidated stock fencing. It was the season of lambing snows, late April, and a drift had nearly covered her. Evidently, she had been there for some time and had gone into labour because out of her backside protruded the head of a lamb, now dead, its eyes pecked out. The ewe barely stirred. I freed her from the fence and walked to a nearby house, where I saw a man sloping off into a barn. I followed him. The barn was filled with the shells of cars of varying vintage. The body of a turquoise jalopy hung from the ceiling on chains. A red sports car was visible beneath some sheeting. The man faced me as I entered, wiping his hands on a rag. I spoke in my native tongue, trying to get across the business about the sheep. The rag continued its progress across the back of his hands. I gestured, and in this I was more successful, for the man looked as if he caught my meaning and became very angry. He shouted words with many syllables in the language that I did not understand. At last, he walked to a desk on the other side of the barn and pulled a phone receiver out from under the detritus of paper, crisp bags, takeaway containers and the like that buried the desk. He began dialling and gestured at me to stay. I could see no way my presence would improve the outcome of the situation. And so I left. It was my first act of deliberate disobedience since arriving in the country, my first and, I silently vowed to myself as I strode out of the barn, my last.

In spite of this assurance, it was soon after this that I noticed that the local suspicion about incomers in general seemed to be directed particularly in my case. I connected this to the incident with the pregnant ewe and knew that I was being held responsible for what had transpired. Although no single or joint complaint was submitted to me or, as far as I knew, to my brother, it was clear even so that I was being accused of wrongdoing, but in a manner and a language I could not understand and so could not address. It was a familiar feeling:

wherever I had been in my life I was always an incomer, an offlander, sometimes a usurper, more rarely a conniver, it was something in my blood that made me feel this way and likewise something in my blood that made others feel this too, that I was strange somehow, not to be trusted. At times this manifested in the usual way; at other times, guilt drove people to magnanimity. Owing perhaps to some discomfort with my ethnic background, as it was called at the time, I was for instance repeatedly made treasurer of organisations for which I worked and volunteered, never mind that I had no experience of handling money or dealing with budgets and rarely had on my person or even in my possession the correct identity cards that would enable me to cash cheques. Nevertheless, eager to prove themselves broadminded, enlightened, perhaps even (they may have whispered, smiling, to themselves) liberal, I was elected to this unsought role of treasurer a number of times over the course of my professional life. I made the best of these appointments, checking my sums on a calculator, endeavouring to become interested in the details everyone assumed were already of the utmost interest to me, small economies, the saving of pennies, the charging of interest. I rarely lasted long in these posts, I would be moved on to another task, my particular skills, never elucidated, needed urgently elsewhere. In other words, I had become accustomed to being an object of slightly sordid, slightly queasy interest and although I took pains to correct the assumptions made about me, by presenting myself meek and clean, pressed and pliable, I rarely was as successful in this as I wished to be.

In the town, for example, I noticed that children had become a source of particular anxiety, perhaps because there were so few of them, all were pupils in the one-room schoolhouse. There was an elaborate system of superstitions regarding these children and their upbringing, so that mothers would often cover the eyes of the infants strapped into strollers if I chanced upon them on the road and ventured a smile. When I walked down the town's main street in the spring sunshine, the lambing snow melting to slush on the pavement, and happened upon a young mother, a woman of perhaps my age, with whom I might in some other life have struck up an acquaintance, even a friendship, out would come the buggy canopy with a dignified pop. Pop, pop, I heard, up and down the main street, as I made my slow and deliberate way, pop, pop. I understood. I noticed that up north, I too had become superstitious. I had my rituals. I denied myself in every possible way. I went for walks, I spoke to no one. When I went into town to do the shopping, a trip I took now every few days, I kept a placid smile on my face, one of my least objectionable expressions, I thought. I knew that, wherever I went, I was being swindled: as far as I could tell, none of the shops marked out the prices of the items for sale, at least not in any of the numerical systems familiar to me, and since I could not ask, I had to be satisfied with whatever amount was rung up by the person at the till. Because I could not understand the language in which any of this happened, however, the sense of shame I was accustomed to feeling was far less acute than in my previous life, and I satisfied myself with that knowledge. I was used to being alone. Since girlhood I had an instinct for retreat, knowing perhaps even then that withdrawing into myself was my only talent, the only way I had and ever would have of exercising any control over the situations in which I found myself in the course of my life, a control that was negligible but nevertheless all I had. My siblings had naturally always supported me in this endeavour, encouraging me to suppress any hint of ambition or even self-love as it arose, my eldest brother in particular had long ago devoted himself to the pursuit of the sacred, which he felt could only be found through the daily mortification of the spirit, mine more often than not, and yet to his credit he worked hard to maintain a sense of shame in himself, it did not come naturally to him as it did to me, that abiding state of disgrace. In a sense, he had said, patting my hand, affliction simplifies everything.

My encounter with the dying ewe and her deceased offspring was the first in a series of unfortunate events that occurred that spring while my brother was away. The year's new life arrived with difficulty, its courage faltering at every step, something I could well understand, the labours and pains of life were familiar to me as they were to most, and then one arrived in the world after expending such tremendous effort only to become one more monstrous bloom in these late days. As I walked through the woods, at times I thought – perhaps after all not everyone wished me ill. And then I would hear a voice inside me say: No, no. Not likely. And I felt an intimacy with these people, I sympathised with them. In truth I knew what they meant. I had never been able to live in my life. Which is not to say I tried to live in anyone else's, merely that from a young age I was heedful, I took instruction easily and tried to live according to the narratives made available to me. With this latter point I struggled. I had difficulty for instance understanding my life in terms of the hero's journey that, according to a documentary I had seen on television in my early teens, characterised the myths and legends that themselves formed the basis of the narratives by which many nations, religions, ethnic groups, tribes, families and even individual people understood themselves. In the first place I was evidently not a main character, had never been of the journeying kind – my present displacement to my brother's home notwithstanding – and neither could I understand myself as guide or magical helper along the way, for frankly what good was I to anyone? For all the trouble I went to for my siblings, for my co-workers, my acquaintances, I had observed that nobody ever did seem any better off for my intervention. I felt this had to do with the vagaries of human suffering, and yet at times I wondered what this might say about me, some spiritual poverty of mine, no doubt, a failure of attention, even though it was my attention, or more precisely and usually my presence at the point of a reckless and personal disclosure, that seemed to be the problem. I said so little and yet it was too much. Much too much. I vowed to make myself smaller and smaller, on numerous occasions throughout my life I had made this same vow, after speaking too rashly in the primary school lunch room or in the high school corridors, I would sit in my bedroom telling myself over and over again, hour after hour, that I would not speak a single word the following day, that I would limit myself in all ways, that I would take up less space.

I thought of a beautiful girl who had collected me when I was sixteen, out of curiosity perhaps, it was only natural that a certain amount of lurid interest had attached itself to me by that point, and I became devoted to this girl, I did whatever she asked, any item of clothing, any accessory she complimented me on I divested myself of immediately, I gave to her, I lived for her, but none of this succeeded in making her love me. She accused me of being perverse, of trying to live in her life, and when at last I withdrew, she pursued me. Across the years she would find me again and make the same accusations, that I had taken her life, stolen her spirit, taken everything from her. I was sure that twenty and more years on, even perhaps someday soon in this remote northern country, she would find me and accuse me of plundering her dreams, ruining any success she might have hoped for, leading off everyone she had ever and might ever have loved, when so far as I knew I had heard nothing of her life for many years, had no idea of the people with whom she associated, the profession she had undertaken, her likes and dislikes, whether she had learned how to drive or draw or whether she had had children. I wished her only happiness and yet I knew that this, too, would be only one more unforgivable thing. Well into adulthood and even with the best will in the world, I still had not mastered the art of the well-tempered refusal, still I was overcome with fits of magnanimity, which visited me suddenly and at inopportune moments, causing any person who had shown me the slightest kindness to feel a swift sense of regret, my rush of generosity overcame them, it could hardly be matched, no response was possible.

Fortunately, as I grew older, these instances became more infrequent. I tried to take myself in hand, it was not goodness I delivered in those moments, goodness, I reminded myself, did not announce itself, goodness was moderate, it submitted. Such were the teachings I remembered from my schooldays, from Traditions class, from the lessons in the workbook provided to us, on the cover of which was a photograph of a baseball player who had, famously, responded to a higher calling. Whenever I recalled my own behaviour, I worked to effect in myself a sense of shame and perhaps even of terror, two small bubbles bobbing up against one another inside me, feeding off one another, becoming more active, becoming malignant, feeding off their host, growing prodigiously in size, pressing against my insides, suffocating, suffocating, and then my breathing would become rapid and shallow and my blood vessels would constrict and I would need to steady myself, and I thought of the desert, which seemed to me an ideal habitat, a habitat so full of nothing, replete with it, a nothing that would settle on one's shoulders and keep one company. Someday, I told myself as I worked to catch my breath, I would withdraw to the desert, why not, who would stop me, to some place in the American Southwest, withdraw to a cave in the hills, a wooden house in a valley, live in silence in among my surroundings, live in contemplation, speaking without knowing it, a new language, the language particular to each being and object on the earth. Yes, I would like that, I thought, imagining myself at the mouth of the cave, sitting on the wooden porch, as I lay in the ornately carved bed in my room in my brother's house, letting as I often did the dream play across my mind. And then, at last, at long last, I would sleep.

4

ON COMMUNITY FARMING

My brother telephoned one morning from a location he did not disclose, evidently he had received word of my imprudent enrolment in community farming, it became apparent during the course of our conversation that he was receiving regular reports on my comings and goings, that a decision had been taken, and he had been asked by those in charge, never named, to translate my tasks to me. Later that afternoon,

I was to present myself at the cowshed, the largest barn, for the purposes of mucking it out, an operation, my brother explained, which involved forking the cows' bedding and manure into one particular corner. The herd, my brother said, had been a small one, fewer than ten, much-loved dairy cows, each with her own name, her own personality, her own allegiances. (O the secret life of cows!) One day, my brother said, the herd had been overtaken by a swift and total madness. They kicked their milkers, they charged the gate, they threw themselves against the walls, roaring and roaring. As a result, the collective of volunteers who ran the community farm came to a consensus – an interesting word, suggesting consent, suggesting its manufacture – that action must be taken, that the cows would have to be culled. There was nothing else for it, it happened so rarely, this kind of collective bovine hysteria, the mass psychogenic illness of the cow. It was agreed that the cows' primary keeper, a shy and tender man in middle-old age, who loved them so dearly, would take their slaughter in hand, all of them, Millie and May, Bluebell and Buttercup and Mayflower, now all dead, all buried in a mass grave behind the barn, a sort of barrow on which daisies had just begun to grow.

The extermination of the herd had taken place several weeks earlier, not long, as it happened, my brother said, after my arrival, and no one had entered the barn since. I liked the idea of the task, clearly defined and solitary, the other hands on the farm that day would be building a chicken run in the yard and part way into the woods; chickens, I would learn in the course of my all too brief apprenticeship, were descended from jungle fowl and enjoyed a thick undergrowth. This chicken run, my brother said, was a source of bad feeling all around, yet another sign of the government, far away in a city somewhere to the south, dictating to the rest of the country how they ought to live, all the while the money, the investment in infrastructure, circulated exclusively in the southern metropolises and certain politically expedient heartland areas. One saw the same thing the whole world over, my brother said, as he had so many times before, I could just see him, tapping the newspaper for emphasis. The Department of Agricultural Affairs and its associated authorities had, to make a long story short, given notice to the keepers of domestic fowl that there had been an outbreak of avian flu in one of the neighbouring nations, a nation which had been, at intervals, ally and enemy, occupier and liberator, and that, as a precautionary measure and for an unspecified length of time, all domestic birds, including but not limited to chickens, geese, pigeons, ducks, etcetera, would have to be protected from their wild sisters and brothers, either in coops or in barns, in runs or in homes. Inspectors would be circulating, fines would be imposed. To that end the chicken run, considered the most humane of the available options, simulating as it did something close to the birds' usual habitat, was to be built. The hens would be able to range, the run would incorporate some of their favourite landscape features, such as tussocks of grass, such as bracken, such as dry patches under particular trees where they liked to scratch and settle, bathe in the dust, clucking happily. Thus, my brother explained, would any townspeople be occupied that afternoon, when I was to present myself for my first volunteer session, all of them far away from the barn, at no risk of seeing me, still less of crossing my path, my brother made it clear that, once I had arrived, I was not to stray from the barn for any reason up until the moment my work was finished and I could return to his house. This I was to do directly, I was to mount my bicycle and ride without stopping, without looking to the right or to the left, without looking behind me, keeping my gaze before me, riding straight back up the road.

After ringing off, I sat down on the terrace, at a small table in the shade of an oak tree that had recently come into leaf and had begun to spread its vast and beautiful crown against the sky. The day felt fresh, I was drinking coffee, eating a croissant I had procured a little while earlier, after much misunderstanding and offence at the town's bakery, while Bert undertook his meditative circuit around the perimeter. It is fair to say we felt good in that moment, we were at one with one another and with our surroundings. It was a rare hour of peace, I felt I had achieved some small thing, the finding of beauty, of solitude, a moment of contemplation at last, and in the daylight hours, before even the hour of dusk which had been, in my old life, the single space of time in which my mind could unspool itself from the demands of the day, the rigours of behaving in accordance with expectations. Contemplation, I knew first hand, was the beginning of devotion: to attend to the people and things of the world had been a practice of living for me, my primary concern in some ways, since I had to apply myself with the utmost seriousness to keep up with my contemporaries so far as social behaviours and mores were concerned. Through these observations I learned that people liked comfort and prosperity, that these were things that were desirable; over the course of the many years nursing my siblings and, when they were present, my parents too, I felt their softness, the essential formlessness of their bodies, the permeability of their flesh, which I feared and also prayed would consume me entire.

My personal preference was for the austere, the walls of my studio apartment in the city had been pale, the furnishings spare, the corners dusted. I liked to sit looking out the window of this apartment, which faced on to a leafy alleyway, my chin resting on the sill so that I could get a sense of the weather, of the city, without being in among either. I knew, indeed had been told, flat out, on many occasions by every one of the members of my family in turn that this was an indulgence, that I was inconsiderate, even selfish, that I was committing sacrilege, for had not the rabbis always said that the Lord did not create the world for desolation, but for human habitation? In this way did my family draw me back to them again and again over the years.

My mildness and complacency were studied, for since girlhood I had wanted to be good, always and still to no avail, I had been marked out for punishment from the start. As a child I had the right answers and wanted to give them, and because of this the teachers found ways to put me in my place, to ensure I was humiliated before my peers, removed from class and perhaps even excluded from the school altogether. With these ends in mind, the teachers deployed all manner of tactics, accusing me of plagiarism, prohibiting me from taking exams, interrogating me before the class on philosophical questions that far exceeded what was covered by the grade school curriculum, and in their efforts they were successful, just as my siblings and to a lesser extent my parents were successful in their similar purpose at home. I put down my hand. I stayed quiet. And I smiled, oh, yes, I smiled. Alone with Bert in my brother's garden, I was determined I would be left alone at last in this splendid place where my fatal hunger for approval would not get the better of me. I sipped my coffee as if to seal the intention, smiled again, placed the cup back on the small wrought-iron table where I sat under the oak tree, and then I looked up.

Before me was a woman and beside this woman, a dog, quite the most exquisite dog, proud and alert with a noble build underneath what was, I had to admit, a very fine coat of tan and black fur. I had not heard the woman enter the garden; to be sure there was no way in except from inside the house, I myself had accessed the garden through the French doors that led from my brother's rococo sitting room. Unless this woman, and this I felt was unlikely, had crawled through the linden hedge, which was looking especially robust in its spring garments, she must have come through the front door, which I had supposed locked, or else through a window, all of which were kept shut, proceeded into the sitting room, thence through the French doors, and managing what's more to do so without my noticing her. Her hair was not in any state of disarray, indeed she looked very tidy and well put together if clearly in a state of fury, which I could not explain since it was she who was trespassing, since I had never seen this woman or her astonishing dog before in my life. Nevertheless, I saw myself sitting there, the usual placid expression on my face, and could well understand her anger. I wanted nothing more than to placate this woman, to set her at her ease, to invite her to sit down for a cup of coffee and, it would be inevitable, to unburden herself to me. Although I knew as the muscles expanded across my face that it would be a mistake, I smiled at the woman. She continued fixing me with a particular look I had grown used to seeing on the faces of the townspeople whenever I encountered them. The dog – a Carpathian Shepherd, I later learned, a rare and courageous breed – stayed perfectly still. The woman was here with a message of some kind, upon an errand anyway, for why else would she be standing before me in my brother's garden on this (it had to be said) spectacular day, and so I waited. I wondered how the interaction would unravel between this woman, one of the townspeople whose existence I had up until this moment never so much as suspected, and me, who had failed to learn to speak or even to understand the most basic phrases of the language of this woman and her people. I waited, I remained silent.

The woman would reveal her meaning, of that I felt sure, she looked very resolute standing there in her yellow shirtwaist dress, very picturesque with the dog beside her, the garden behind and around her in its springtime dress, she looked as though she belonged here. O suns! I thought. O grass of graves! For I had been reading poetry that morning in the garden and was exultant still. I felt as though I might weep for the beauty of it all, for the vanishing world. In another life, this woman and I might have shared our nightmares over coffee some morning. Only in another life, yes, yes. Whatever there was in me that I knew was part of the problem but could not name, nor pin down precisely, nevertheless I knew it was in me. But History too was part of the problem, I reflected. I felt that the towns-people, in spite of my brother's respectability, in spite of the power of ownership he availed himself of, knew what we were, where we had come from, a place that once existed on the other side of the forest, that was now only whispered about. I would have liked to tell this woman that I had no desire to rise above my kind, that I would, if I could, sink into the pit on the other side of the forest, that someday I would find my way back there and never return, never be seen again. Alas I could not communicate this complex sentence, could not convey these abstractions, these morbidities, not least because it could not make her trust me more, no, and not when I could not even form the word *hello*. Hello, I said out loud, startling myself. The woman turned pale. Pale – but why did she turn pale? What was there to fear, here in the garden? I had not set upon her in the minutes that had elapsed since I discovered her trespassing on my brother's property, there was no reason to suppose I would do so now. What was there to fear from me, the most benign, the most insipid, person in the area, notably weak and small of frame?

Upon closer inspection, I realised the fantastic dog, who sat so serenely there beside her mistress, was pregnant. Was this then why the woman had come? Something to do with the dog's pregnancy – to sell a puppy, perhaps? As if hearing my thoughts, the woman nodded. She pointed to Bert, who had chosen this moment to urinate on a preferred bush. Bert? I said. The woman nodded again, then pointed to her own dog. She went on in this way for some time, articulating other, more obscure gestures. Over time I began to grasp her meaning. The woman had been led to believe, for what reason or by whom I could not tell, that Bert had impregnated her magnificent dog. Of course, she could not know about Bert's difficult medical history, the removal of his testicles, the loss of one of his legs, nevertheless, and anyway, he had never so far as I knew ventured outside the confines of the house and gardens, certainly not long enough to mate with this strange dog, whom I was sure neither Bert nor I had ever seen. No, no, I said to the woman. Yes, yes, she nodded. There would be no dissuading her, I saw that, of course, I realised, it was money she was after, I reached for my handbag, which hung on the back of my chair, and withdrew a couple of bills. This did not please her, but it did bring the encounter to an end, since, after speaking a few quiet and dignified words, unintelligible of course to me, she turned and disappeared from the garden.

The whole situation was so incomprehensible that I forgot all about it almost immediately upon the woman's departure. I went into the house to heat up my coffee and returned to the sun in the garden. Nothing seemed to have changed in the house, in the garden, on the terrace, nothing was disarranged, but it was as though my sensations had become heightened. My breath rang in my ears, the pumping of blood through my body, some sudden unreadable urge: urge and urge and urge. How curious. It was connected to that thrill of fear I had felt emanating from the woman. Nobody before had found me frightening. I had never before been conscious of having made any kind of imprint on anyone, had never so far as I was aware aroused any substantial emotions or reactions, except perhaps that placeless and silent loathing of the underdog that I have already described.

I went into the house to change for the afternoon's work, making sure Bert was comfortable in his bed beneath the kitchen table, and I cycled down the road. The day had clouded over, the light now harsh and bright, but the cooler air had a wetness in it that felt pleasant on my skin. I wanted so badly to live in my life, wanted to meet it head on, wanted above all for something to happen, for this terrible yearning to be quenched. What was underneath it all, vibrating beneath the faces of the people I saw, something in their expressions? What howls restrained there, by decorum, by cowardice, for fear of sinking? I was moved by the trees that lined the road, reaching over and across, towards one another. The crowns of birches, of oaks and elms, all rolling against the sky, flashing up their pale undersides in the wind, how was it that very thing brought me so low? It was only a tree in springtime, only the memory of sitting in the empty bleachers behind the high school, still a girl, feeling as if my skin would burst open, but nothing, nothing ever happened. It was not a message or an omen. It was not loneliness. What, then? What was this air one breathed?

In the cowshed, everything had been prepared for me, there was nothing I needed to ask, all the tools I might require had been put at my disposal, the section of the barn which would accommodate the muck heap had been clearly marked out with what looked like block-ing tape stuck to the floor. I got to it. It was physically demanding work but pleasurable for that, although I tried to control the satisfaction I derived from what was after all a sad but necessary task, a task any number of working people had engaged in before, not, like me, as hobbyists, but by coming to it honestly. Nevertheless, my mind felt clear. In a few weeks it would be midsum-mer, a date whose significance I felt deeply but which I always failed somehow to bring into being. In other years I had spent it drinking wine on a café terrace in the city, trying to take in that distinctive blue in the air, sitting in silence. I knew each year I had come up short once again without really knowing why or what to do about it. The last of the lengthening days, soon the wind would pick up, everything would be over, the long, long winter settling in. I had hoped that here in the country I would experience the turn of the seasons differently, with less apprehension, I might come to see the form and plan of the world. Not to frame it within systems of understanding, of domination, no, I would work to allow the world its right to illegibility, to move in darkness.

To take shape in its contact with people but to remain essentially itself. In the country, I would overcome this final difficulty at last, renounce my will to knowledge, give up my attachment to expression, and in this way come to understand the meaning of things.

I worked through the afternoon in the cool barn, I worked through the evening and into the night, even a herd of fewer than ten cows could produce a substantial amount of mess, I learned, and so I heaped the muck high. I sluiced the concrete floor with buckets of water, swept it clean with a long-handled broom. When I was finished, I cleaned all the implements. I was meticulous. Even I, who knew so little, knew something about diseases and their transmission. I shut off the overhead lights. I pulled the doors to. It went without saying I hoped my efforts would prove something to the townspeople, about my will to service, that I wanted to build bridges, that finally I consented to my role and responsibility in our shared history, a role whose outlines I had only then dimly imagined.

The dog and her mistress never again entered my brother's garden, but every Saturday morning in the weeks that followed they held vigil under one of the pine trees on the drive. They stood, immobile, for a number of hours and always departed before dusk. As the pregnancy matured, the dog's mistress became increasingly agitated. Sometimes I would see her rocking back and forth on the balls of her feet, eyes closed, whispering to herself, the dog at heel. I too became distressed. I knew that Bert was incapable of copulating with, still less impregnating, any dog at all, even the most fertile, at the peak of her season, no, of this I knew he was incapable, but still I remained on edge. I went on the Internet to ascertain the length of a dog's gestation period, a matter I learned of some sixty to seventy days, approximately two to two and a half months. The animal had already been visibly pregnant when they visited in early May, it could not have more than four or five weeks to go, and I awaited the results of its whelping with apprehension. In the meantime, the townspeople had been satisfied with my performance in the cowshed, and I had been assigned, via my brother, to a further series of tasks which I undertook in the weeks leading up to the dog's due date.

As I spent more time outside, undertaking the tasks of late spring and early summer, I felt the days unspooling behind me and before me, I sensed the way the year rolled on through its own traces. It was something I had seldom felt. My experience of continuity had been limited to the way each new catastrophe sat in the last, as if it had already happened and would go on happening, on and on. And so I lived in the historical rupture of the present, in the historical aberration of my life, and I submitted to those that had me at their mercy in an effort to soften their hearts. But now, for the moment, things were well. I had found a way to serve the community, in silence and at a distance (for had not the sages said that good deeds are better done in anonymity, without gratitude?), in my brother's absence I had found some form for the days. If in the preceding weeks I had loved too well my walks among the budding trees of the forest, if I had felt the smallest temptation to withdraw my obedience, I knew that once again I had to gain mastery over myself, over the motions of my spirit, various and vain.

And yet there remained this matter of the dog. I believed in truth, and yet if I had learned anything in life it was that in the world of creation, nothing stayed still; everything was becoming and dissolving. What I knew about Bert's sterility was a veterinary fact, perhaps even a biological one, but I acknowledged that this was only one way of seeing things. The woman had, doubtless, her own worldview, one that was evidently incompatible with mine but no less true, according to its own internal rules. Perhaps my adherence to one particular outlook was further evidence of my failure to root out the terrible pride my eldest brother and all the siblings in between had warned me of. The episode was a useful reminder of the essential weakness and debility of my own nature. After some reflection, I decided that I was happy to accept her version of events, since after all she was much more credible than I was, at the very least more assured. I would tell her so the following week, I decided, when next she and the dog came to stand in the drive. I was calm then. I felt happy. I would give the woman what she wanted. I would accede. I had done well to interrogate my own motives, I thought. I had approached the edge of something. I scraped the walls of the chicken shed, I scraped the roosts, I turned the straw. I rode back up the hill on my bicycle, without looking left, without looking right.

The days passed quickly, one disappearing into the next, and all around me the world changed, the green world quickening. On the Saturday I rose early and took a cup of coffee into the garden. I felt a pleasurable soreness in my shoulders and arms. I had spent the night before cleaning, washing, waxing, the house was spotless and smelled of almonds. Sitting in the garden, I reflected on the space, its public and private faces and the relationship between the two. What kind of self came into view in a space like a garden, where one was on one's brother's private property, and yet in full view of anyone who happened to pass by? The distinction between the two spheres, public and private, had been an insoluble problem over the course of my upbringing, particularly during my teenage years, but even before that, yes, much earlier than that. In my parents' home – my home, after a fashion – I was always on view, my appearance much commented on, my state of disarray, physical or emotional, remarked on and discussed, any desires or proclivities I had thought secret were unearthed without difficulty and shared without scruple. The situation was the same in among the extended family, I observed, and so too in gatherings of the community at large. This intelligence was used as social currency, a way for the speaker to force an intimacy with someone at no cost to their own dignity; the elected member was often in fact present at the disclosures, held as a sort of hostage in the complex social interaction where everyone feigned good cheer. Yes, yes, that kind of heartiness was familiar to me, it was never in short supply at any of these gatherings, weddings or funerals, naming ceremonies or ritual circumcisions, where in each corner of any given room stood these arrangements of three people: one with an avuncular arm around the shoulder of a second, standing stiffly, and a third bent forward with a conspiring half-smile playing about the mouth. I had stood in these groupings myself, listened as my most cherished, my most dearly held, most intimate thoughts were articulated by a distant relative or one-time acquaintance, usually to a total stranger, and we all laughed together. How we laughed. It was part of my training, I understood that now, my uncommon pride and self-love which needed to bend, needed to be subdued, and it was of some comfort to me to see that there were others who faltered similarly, who needed the guiding hand of semi-public shame. I understood this even then as part of the process of community formation, of the operations of power and the delegation of roles, who and what lay beyond describing the outlines of whatever lay within. It was the late twentieth century. What did we have left? A prayer book, some scraps of song, a history lesson beginning with devastation.

I decided to do some transcription work in the garden as I waited for the woman. I pressed an earbud into my left ear, leaving the right empty lest I should miss the sound of her arrival, and began typing. I began to develop a kind of aversion to my work around this time. I was making mistakes, typing more slowly, breaking paragraphs in strange places and neglecting the use of the full stop. Up to then, writing had been an exercise in fidelity: transcribing exactly what I heard within the parameters of a strict grammatical framework. Semicolons were to be used sparingly and to separate two independent clauses joined by a conjunctive adverb or else to separate items in a list where those items themselves contained commas. All other uses were to be avoided. Such was the house style. I had prided myself on a well-placed comma, a clarifying colon. It had always been a delight to me to take the vocalisations of my colleagues and organise them according to the immutable laws of grammar, turn them into the purest, most crystalline utterances. And yet, and gradually, my adherence to these rules dropped off. I became more interested in the sound of my colleagues' sentences, the shape of their words, the occasional and probably unintended sibilance, the repetitions and elisions, the hesitations or pauses where the grammar did not mandate them. I found new ways to mark these idiosyncrasies, making use of space on the page. It seemed to me a truer notation of the language than how I had proceeded up to that point. The revision in my approach had been slow and creeping, so far no one had remarked upon it, and it occurred to me for the first time that my colleagues might not actually make any use of these documents that I was employed to type out. I had not imagined my work was of any particular importance, of course not,

merely quietly helpful, enabling my colleagues to produce pieces of paper at key moments in legal research,
at trials, that they might point to and say: there. That
was all. I thought of the lawyer, incarcerated in his own
home, sitting on the sofa in sweatpants, scratching at his
ankle monitor. What use was knowledge? Any scrap of
information one could want was at one's disposal now,
all the means of modernity employed to root out the
smallest factoid, but it had not done him or anyone else
any good. One always seemed to fall into the hands of
a judge who was also one's enemy. No plunder too low,
no picking too slim. One's very ashes would be sifted
for the gold tooth, the wedding ring. What was it that
I was thinking of? Something about the world and its
vain promise of the present. Why had I believed in it?
Choice, the individual, the world and what it made possible on the one hand; and us, the family, on the other.
For my parents, the world out there would never be the
world they knew, that could never be put back, no. But
as for myself, I recognised in the end something behind
the brand-newness of the world, a shadow just visible
beneath its seams. Here I was, sitting in my brother's

garden, after all that effort, all those years, nothing any different, the underlying ideology adapting again and again to each liberation as it presented itself. The faces changed, sure they did, but ways of doing just persist, all one's born days. What else is there to say?

I noticed that neither the woman nor her dog had arrived though the sun had begun to move away from its noontime height. I rose from my chair and stretched, feeling the sun on my skin, feeling as if I were living by favour extraordinary and had been for some time. After all, the woman was nothing to do with me, it was only that I had grown used to seeing her standing there under the row of pines. If the woman could give up her vigil, which had seemed so enduring – seemed indeed to have endured so many months, though it could not have been more than a matter of weeks – what could I not give up? How ineluctable the paths one treaded! And yet if something could happen, was indeed ever happening, did it not then follow that nothing, too, could happen? One might, in later years, develop an ability to pull up short, to stop at last and sit down on the path, one had grown weary, one's feet become sore, the boots worn through.

Perhaps after all I was beginning to let go of this inhuman fixing, the freezing into expression. My senses had been dulled by the abiding nature of the world's provocations, and I knew that my habits and usual practices would be difficult to break. What remained of me, after a life of service? One tried and failed to retain one's integrity through a bad education, I reflected; one had been trained in certain ways which, with some distance and hindsight, one might come to see as unhealthy, if not utterly depraved. I had not yet, not on that day in the garden, not in the light of the westering sun – for the day indeed was beginning to wane – acquired the ability to think again. Nevertheless, something had transpired, I had at the very least encountered the concept of habit and understood that custom too had its point of origin.

5

A PRIVATE RITUAL

When my brother returned a few weeks later, I would learn the outline of what happened to the dog. What elsewhere would have been merely ridiculous was treated in the town and surrounding areas as a tragic incident but primarily and clearly an occult one. What I mean by this is that the dog's phantom pregnancy, alluded to in the opening lines of this account, was understood by the townspeople to have been brought to pass by means covert and malignant, the event and the form of the event a terrible calamity. They were an earthly people, not particularly given to affairs of the spirit, but something came over the towns-people that spring and summer, strange things had been happening, and they would not reach their pinnacle with the affair of the dog, no, and not for a while. I could well understand how the series of misfortunes with regard to the local animal life must have seemed connected, how, added together, they might appear to constitute a concerted, organised or even divine pun-ishment. And yet I did not quite perceive that a cloud of discontent had begun to roil over the town. There were certain indications, signs I would have been able to read had I been paying attention. A sense of things fraying. Yes, strange things had been happening in the countryside, in the blue gloaming of the early hours, at one in the morning, at two or three, sometimes at four and a few times as late as five o'clock, I would hear intermittent blasts, like those caused, for instance – or so I supposed, having never heard the noise in real life, only in films and on television, and so could not be sure, exactly, given the added degree of depth, the specific topographical layout that might catch sound or cause it to reverberate, cause it to echo – by the discharge of a gun. On several occasions I found the skinned remains of eviscerated rabbits in the garden, by the woodpile, on the front step. I figured a polecat, or a mink, or a weasel, a particularly voracious one, or else a colony of several who had established themselves somewhere nearby and found a safe place in my brother's garden to devour their really quite prolific spoils, and I dutifully cleared away the masses of these leavings, dutifully, yes. I have already mentioned the thrice-daily practice of the local dogs, in which even Bert, who normally was so docile, so (how else to explain it) undoglike, who I would have thought above such affairs, participated, rounding his little mouth and howling the most terrible, the most heart-wrenching lament three times each day. Each of these things I explained away with ease – it was hunting season, there were undoubtedly predators in the woods, the solstice had come and gone and the summer days were beginning to take on a different texture, things drying up and diminishing, and one felt it, one felt it just as the dogs felt it, the sadness of the passing days, the melancholy of autumn approaching, it was only the strangeness peculiar to the time of year, the disruption, the death one felt in the air and in oneself, the swift contraction of the days acting as a reminder of all the things one had overlooked, one had forgotten, and now the time for those things had passed, it was too late, far, far too late.

Once, walking in the woods late that summer, I crossed paths with the woman and her dog. They did not see me. Although I cut across their path, sometimes following behind them, even at times walking beside them, they appeared neither to hear nor to see me. The dog did not catch my scent. They merely walked on, the dog expressing drops of milk as they went. As far as I could tell, they were not sick, they did not appear weak, progressing through the woods and up the hill silently, unbent, with unflagging steps; nor did they appear to have become suddenly or especially mad, but only to have moved somewhere beyond the present. They were silent and distant. I liked them this way, even to tell the truth preferred this new state of theirs. To be alongside a person as entirely other, unreadable, intact – as an equal – it was a gift. I beheld it then and remembered it for a long time after. It gave me a secret strength, which I thought had shown itself for the first time in my decision to accede to the woman's accusations, to agree with them wholeheartedly, to go along with her, yes, sometimes I thought it was this moment which had actually precipitated the languid and faraway state into which she and her dog had retreated. For was it not the case that, having been pressed into the knowledge of their situation entirely against their will, forced into a way of knowing that was not theirs, this woman and her dog could only have been suffering in the most profound state of abjection? And, when one looked at it a certain way, had I not caused this state to come to pass, created the conditions for its arrival by only pretending to accept, thereby refusing, this woman's right to an essential separateness, her essential reality? Had I not precipitated this state of being that was, so much became clear to me when I saw the woman and her dog walking through the forest, actually just what I myself had been striving towards? For no consolation was possible for the woman, for the dog, no consolation would ever now be possible, even were it offered, not in this world. She had been thrust out of herself by a structure of thought that hailed us all, sooner or later, and to which I worked to subject myself my whole life long. Did it follow, then, that I had achieved some measure of grace, after all? That, after all this time, and completely unbeknownst to myself, I had passed into the role of a teacher, a kind of spiritual guide, whose own motions of the spirit were so powerful as to be able to influence the thought and action of others? No, no, surely not, I reflected, giving Bert, who had crept on to my lap, a scratch behind the ears. Nothing could have induced me to take on a leadership role of any kind, I was a faithful and perennial servant, and yet, and no one could have found the situation more impossible than I did, it seemed to me that my obedience had itself taken on a kind of mysterious power. And if I had been granted this power, by some grace, against my wishes, must I not then make use of it in some way? Such were my thoughts as I continued to caress Bert's ears, as he snored peacefully on my lap having fallen asleep some way into my ruminations which, I learned on looking at the clock, had gone on for several hours, it was nearly morning, very close to the witching hour as we used to call it as children. I became anxious, feeling that I had been wasting time, that as soon as I had suspected my new-found power I ought to have begun putting it to use. Was an intervention possible? I thought of the townspeople and their private rituals, they and I both pulled along by the unseen forces of history. I took Bert up in my arms and climbed the stairs to bed.

The next morning I found myself standing by the petrol pump outside the café. The sky hung low and grey over the car park, throwing no shadow, making the edges of everything sharp and clear. Inside the café, the business of the morning. Why after all disturb them, I thought, turning away, why force the contact? Two dots never meeting, never meaning to meet. And yet, I told myself, one might take a first step. One might establish the conditions for a reconciliation, I thought, opening the door of the café. The usual tinkling bell, the usual sudden silence, the very walls of the café seeming to swallow the words of the townspeople as they watched me cross the threshold. I thought of the entrances of my teenage years, the exits, the collectively held breath that attended these arrivals and leave-takings. At times I comforted myself with the thought that my position enabled the connection of others, my exclusion a service undertaken in the interests of community cohesion. And this, I told myself, looking around the café, this after all was not so very different. In fact, I reflected, these people might be my family, so similar were they to my brother, to our immediate family so far as I could remember them, in colouring, in bone structure, in the sparseness of their hair. Was that not one of my brothers, sitting by the window? And there, at the counter, that older couple: were those not my parents? I slid into one of the booths. A young mother seated at an adjacent table turned her child's perambulator to face away from me. I observed the solemn faces of the café-goers, their right hands twitching in their laps, unconsciously forming the sign, I could just make it out, of a cross. And yet, I thought now, as I had thought at other times, was it not possible that none of this had anything to do with me at all, that the silence of the assembled people predated my arrival and would continue after I was gone, that each couple, each group of friends, had merely fallen into silence, separately and at the same time, silences that were after all only natural in the course of a conversation, over the course of long friendship. Was not the antagonism I had long imagined merely rather a projection of my own inflated sense of self-importance, I said to myself, feeling on more comfortable footing now. I looked down at the place setting, everything aligned just so, the paper mat, the paper napkin, I took pleasure in the symmetry while I awaited the server. Somewhere in the back of the café a radio was going. Otherwise, silence. Eventually a youngish man edged towards the booth. He wore an unspeakable apron and kept his gaze fixed on a point somewhere beyond my left ear. I had prepared myself for this. I pointed to the young mother's coffee cup, and then back to myself. The mother burst into tears. For this too I had been prepared. I persevered, pointing to the counter, whereupon sat a cherry pie under a glass cloche, and then back to myself. The young man waited a moment, seemingly to ascertain whether further instruction was forthcoming, and, receiving none, crept away. Did I not have a right to a cup of coffee, a slice of pie? What after all had I ever done wrong? And if these people resembled my family so closely as to be basically interchangeable with them, did they not then resemble me, too? What was there to mark me out especially? At this point, the young man emerged from behind the counter, holding a cup of coffee cupped between both palms. He walked very slowly, one foot and then the other, his eyes on the lip of the cup, the liquid barely moving, the eyes of the townspeople fixed upon him, I felt for this young man, so diligent, so careful, I knew well how difficult it was to carry a drink over to a table without spilling its contents, without losing the feeling in one's hands and dropping the drink, dropping a plate, dropping a tray, I had done it myself many times before. I watched with bowed head as he placed the cup down on the table before me. I felt a brief release of tension pass through the café. The young man retreated behind the counter, emerging a moment later with the plate of pie. This he managed more easily. With the utmost care, he placed the slice of pie down on the table but, due to an unlucky tremor of the fingers, a sudden loss of faith, the plate was propelled a few inches further than he had intended, directly into the salt shaker, causing the latter to fall on to its side. An easy mistake, and another one I had made so very many times myself, I thought, reaching forth, righting the cellar, throwing a pinch of salt over the left shoulder, an automatic gesture, an old habit, learned at the Sabbath table. The young mother emitted, and then suppressed, a scream. The server fled behind the counter. The hands of the other diners, briefly stilled in their laps during the service, resumed their motions with renewed fervour. I broke into the pie. I watched the steam rise from the coffee. I looked out the window on to the shadowless day. Muscle memory, then, was that what marked me out? Tradition? What was it they thought of, the townspeople, when they saw me walking the streets of their town? What was it they remembered?

It had been a mistake to come, I understood that now. The diner had none of the pleasures I had imagined, not the satisfaction of anonymity, not the joys of the Bunn coffee makers I remembered from childhood or the free refills that came along with them; smoking, even here, had been banned indoors. And instead of ingratiating myself with the townspeople as I had hoped to do, arriving in the diner with my hair brushed, a bit of makeup carefully applied, wearing plain and modest clothing, I had done the opposite, inflaming their superstitions, bringing out their fears, my gesture with the salt meant to reverse the server's bad luck clearly taken as injurious. I looked around. Eggs stood cold and untouched on the plates of the other diners, resting alongside a few dried-out strips of bacon. Everyone it seemed had stopped eating on my arrival, or had never started, worried, I could tell, that in opening their mouths, in swallowing the runny egg, the bit of toast, whatever contagion they associated with me would attach itself to them, following the masticated food down the throat, into the stomach, lodging somewhere in the intestine which, everyone knew, was the seat of bad feeling and ill health. For a moment, I wished it had. I had done enough. I left a few bills on the table and rose to leave.

The sun had come out. I walked the town's sidewalks for a time, observing the way my shadow swung round as I changed direction, as the sun followed its slow, aestival arc. I sat in the town square, I walked past the playground, I looked through the chain-link fence at the municipal pool. Everywhere that same blank look. A few hours passed, it was coming on late afternoon when I found myself standing on a path outside the church. I followed it round to where it terminated at the church-yard, a lovely green and wooded place. The graves were well tended, even the oldest tombstones in good shape. I wondered whether the local tombstone company helped to maintain the grounds, in exchange, perhaps, for a monopoly on the memorials, whose designs were uniformly simple and poignant. So many years of the town's dead lay here, unmolested, in good shape, each townsperson, I imagined, could come here to visit even the most distant of their ancestors, centuries removed. A single, unbroken line into the past. Perhaps that was the essential difference between me and these people, the tangible threads of time that held them fast to this earth, to one place, that entitled them to live and to go on living. What blood feeds a soil like that? Overhead, the leaves trembled in the breeze.

I had reached the far end of the churchyard, where a gate let out on to a flight of wooden steps that ran down a ravine to one of the town's rivers. My brother had explained that some part of the place name reflected the point of convergence of all these waterways, where they clove across one another before running on, certainly, in different directions. As I placed my hand on the gate, I noticed movement down by the river. I stilled my hand and watched. A group of the townspeople, some of whom I now recognised as the shopkeeper, the server, the young mother, the garage owner and a few others, strangers still to me, were gathered at the river's edge. Each of these people held something in their arms, they held, and I could hardly believe it myself, the grass talismans I had woven with so much care and attention. A man I did not recognise – the preacher, perhaps? or priest? what word did they use here? – spoke a few indistinct words. The rest responded as a group. Someone handed him a spade, and he began to dig into the soil upon which they all stood. He dug for a long time, deeply, a hole whose edges met at right angles, just so. By the time he had finished it was getting dark, and I felt the stiffness in my body, in my hand that rested still on the gate. Hours must have passed. The others helped the preacher out of the ground. He wiped his brow, straightened himself, and uttered a single, unintelligible word. The rest turned as one and flung the grass dolls into the pit. They took it in turns to throw shovelfuls of the silty soil on top of the dolls, one by one, until the hole was filled once more, until it had become a small mound. The group stood in silence, in the twilight, with their heads bowed.

It was a perplexing ritual, so laden with potential meaning it was difficult to discern whether it might constitute a blessing or a curse. I worked through the symbology. The proximity to the water, was that life? Wisdom? Undifferentiated chaos? A purifying ritual, of course, of course. But if purifying, why bury the dolls, why not merely submerge them? Why not throw them into the river, allow them to be taken out and away to some far estuary of the world? Too much to hope, I supposed, that the timing of this ritual, so soon after my visit to the café, was merely coincidental. It was clear either way that the townspeople had decided, for how could they do otherwise, that I had been responsible for the mysterious and threatening appearance of the dolls. For what townsperson could have done such a thing, could have hidden a thing like that? Impossible. The gate creaked underneath my hand, and the townspeople, so far down the darkened ravine, too far out of earshot surely to be affected by such a small sound, turned to look up. I dropped my hand and ran, I cannot explain why, ran down the churchyard path, ran up the main street, ran by all the large and beautiful clapboard houses on the town's outskirts, ran under a row of ancient oak, all the way back up the road to my brother's house.

I had hoped, as I have said, that my efforts at the community farm, in making me more visible in the town, might have overwritten some of the bad feeling I sensed had been gathering against me. I had just begun to feel it, pressing at the edges of my brother's property, a mustering of ill will, but after my visit to the café it seemed to take on a more distinct shape, something palpable reaching out to grab hold as I ran and ran. Once safely inside the house, I locked the door and shuttered all the windows. From then on, I told myself, I would perform various rituals to ward off the evil eye, rituals taught to my siblings and me by our mother, one of the few concrete things she had passed down to us, almost by accident. I learnt by observing in any case, observing her, for instance, at the glass in the bathroom, her sadness and her lassitude. Yes, I learned much incidentally and by observing the people around me. That evening, I fed Bert and I retired early to my room.

Nothing had happened, I told myself, no catastrophe, no untimely encounter. I was fine, I thought, pressing my face into the pillow, I was whole. All might still be well. Perhaps all manner of things might after all be well.

And yet my mind reeled. I was unable to sleep, unable to silence the thoughts which presented themselves, unbidden and at all hours. Accepting that my arrival had coincided with the madness and necessary extermination of the cows, the demise of the ewe and her nearly born lamb, the dog's phantom pregnancy, the containment of domestic fowl, a potato blight which I have so far neglected to mention – acknowledging that all these events had occurred in quick succession more or less upon my arrival in the place, and admitting that not one of these things had happened singly in recent memory, that the town and surrounding areas had actually lived through a blessed and prosperous fifty years, and that these unfortunate events had still less ever, in recorded history, happened simultaneously – granting all this, yes, still, it was difficult for me to accept the bad feeling of the townspeople. However hard I toiled at the community farm, however many muckheaps shovelled, however many chicken coops scraped down, however many nettles pulled up by the roots, hung to dry or boiled for soup, still I felt their hostility. All these efforts, I realised with a great sadness, had been in vain, had in all likelihood been doomed from the outset. They had not gained me citizenship in the place; I remained, as I now understand I must always remain, outside. Nevertheless, in the days after I witnessed the burial of the dolls, I continued to present myself at the community farm. No one objected, and I would not have understood even if they had. I wanted so badly to right things before my brother returned, wanted to show him how I had things in hand, how I had behaved correctly, how I had been obedient. I went so little beyond myself, practised a strict economy of hope and communicated no desire to myself or to others. I did all this without seeking any praise, without any self-love, without even (it must be said) much effort or will and yet, I admit, with perhaps a slight degree of avidity, one might say rapacity, even, looked at a certain way, an unsightly if clumsy fanaticism. In spite of all this, all these efforts, I felt radiating from the landscape, surely as ever now, the anger of the townspeople, who after all could not help but think historically, and who, having been in a sense exiled from the modern world to their own home town, a town like any other, whose people had behaved like those in any other, who thus understood the need for roots, whose continued existence depended on this understanding, depended in fact on the pact of silence, on groping, blindly, for the future, saw me as nothing more than a stranger of a fixed, old age, who had appeared out of nowhere to herald, perhaps even bring about, a truly inauspicious time. I was so different to my brother, could hardly be related to him, had perhaps been collected in childhood as a servant waif by a soft-hearted father away on business, only to appear in the township in these too-late days, yes, in order to make them look at themselves, take a long, hard look at their wretched selves, slaves to the past, slaves to their ancestral hatreds, who had lived for so long, for a time anyway, in blithe forgetfulness, in the beautiful rush of the seasons, finding refuge in an earlier way of being, skipping right over the cold and terrible machine age into the distant past, drawing then a line from that much beloved past directly to the present. Things remained ever the same, I thought, sitting on the terrace in the afternoon sun, Bert in my lap. Only the names of things changed, from time to time, from place to place, moving according to whatever was expedient, whatever might affirm the beliefs held by a given people, by a given person, beliefs one needed to hold about oneself, stories one told oneself in order to live, to go on living with oneself, knowing what one was capable of, knowing the things one had witnessed, the things one had done.

In retrospect, from my present vantage point, I can see that all this, taken together with my brother's sudden and unexplained disappearance so soon after my arrival (for so it must have seemed to any onlooker), considering too my new habit of hanging nettles and other plants, hanging chamomile flowers, to dry from the walls of the town's barn, in such great profusion, in truth positively covering every available inch of wall, communicated perhaps a very particular aesthetic that may have tried the patience of the townspeople, though of course I did not see this with such clarity at the time. As far as I was concerned, I was parsimonious, remained resolutely within my own circumference, and because of this I could cast no shadow, I did not see myself reflected in the bearings or mien of any other. This was no curious thing. I had always been susceptible to the desires of other people, any strong feeling experienced in close proximity to me I reflected, like the still surface of a pond at dawn, fathomless, untenanted, so often coming to live these feelings as though they were my own. In the case of the townspeople, although they kept their physical distance, so powerful was the sentiment, so critical the mass, that at times I was overcome, it worked on me, and I lay down on the ground, on the floor of the barn. All of my senses were taken over in these moments and what I could hear, so clearly, were the words that had followed me my whole life long: *Lie down little dog, lie down at last.* And

I would. I would lie down, only to get back up again after a few moments, the stone flags of the barn so hard, the grass outside so wet or so cold, in spite of myself, I would keep on and on, as I had before, as I would continue to do in future, for no rhyme or reason, with no encouragement whatsoever, I would keep on, a perfect specimen of bare life, better off, no doubt, and as had been repeatedly suggested to me, out of it all, put out of my misery, creeping into some earthen hole somewhere never to return. But to my everlasting regret I lacked the genius of self-annihilation and, out of some animal cunning crouched somewhere deep inside of me, I carried on my career of hopeless survival, not undisturbed and surely having exhausted the mercy of providence, such as it was. It was not wisdom, no. I just continued to scrape at the sky.

But my brother was to return and I knew that the impulses that were just beginning to disclose themselves would have to be checked, they would have to be tucked back in. In preparation for his arrival, I got back into his routine. I rehearsed the steps of the morning, the opening up, the airing out, and then those of the closing down and curtaining of the evening. I cleaned each piece of silverware meticulously. I shined the brasses in the kitchen. I laundered the soft furnishings. And before long, there he was, coming up the drive in the same car in which he had driven me from the airport to the house. I thought he looked well, at any rate he looked as though he were in control of the vehicle, he drove with purpose, he had a tan, was probably wearing cologne. I was devoted to him, yes. I opened the driver's-side door, I helped him out, how elegant he looked in his light suit, I told him, brushing the travel from his shoulders. I followed him into the house, carrying his holdall, pursued him into the kitchen, pressed him into a seat, served him a drink, offered the small morsels of refreshment I had prepared, mindful of my brother's tastes and of the challenges posed to the digestive tract of one who has been long travelling. I pushed in his chair, I asked about his work. I felt he was flattered by the attention, that he tucked in gratefully. After this small repast we went out into the garden, the late afternoon sun goldening everything. I brought drinks out on a tray, I lit his cigarette. If at times I detected a slight suspicious cast in my brother's glance, in his aspect, as though my attentions were insincere, as if there existed in me some obscure motivation, I simply bowed my head, lowered my voice, sweetened my look. By the end of that first afternoon I had regained his confidence, he was satisfied with my service and we sat happily alongside one another. We kept to his routine, talking together in the drawing room in the allocated evening hours, as he read the papers, as I read my book, as the television droned in the background, as Bert dozed in front of the fire. He was energetic, in control, and I was content.

I forgot all about the grasses and their growing. I forgot about the night woods, the several woven amulets placed so tenderly on doorsteps and in haylofts, in naves and on cobbles, lying buried now underneath the silt by the river. I had reached out, something I never ought to have done, reached out over that unthinkable abyss of history, but to whom, and in expectation of what, I could not say. I turned back to my project of self-improvement, the searching for the unit of illumination, the never finding it, never stirring from the field of the possible, such were the operations of the doomed inquiry into the soul, the pursuit of a state of gravity and grace.

6

THE OCCASION OF A BROTHER

It was not I should say as though I had been born without questions. I had a youth, like anyone else, and like anyone else had learned to conceal those impulses and behaviours I found to be undesirable to those around me. There had been a time, in my twenties, when I had pursued life and its disclosures, had wanted to help, and so I sat quietly on the end of the line, receiving the most abominable stories in the dead of night, a resource binder on my lap, providing what relief I could, deficient though I clearly was, guiding the breathing of a stranger sitting in distress elsewhere in the city, feet on the ground, wrapped in a blanket, eyes closed, five to eight shifts a month for two years, the hanging up, the never knowing, the emergency room calls. I never did have a horse's ability to pull up short, I walked straight on, yes, in this case straight into silence. One had one's limits, for instance a fourteen-year-old girl in a hospital bed. After that of course the ordinary goings-on in one's workplace, the persecution, the leveraging, the official channels of complaint that navigated one swiftly and directly to a failure of will, the men concerned well versed in libel law, what constituted malice; merely knowing brought one up against the wall in employment matters, over and over again, one heard the stories, there was nothing left but to make an exit, straight on through the cloud. It was that same low-down old story about the commonsensible and the people who get to define it. One kept one's boots on, yes, yes, I have said that already. Eventually I too pulled my hat down over my ears, for what did it all add up to, this world full of possibility? The whisper network put paid to by a line manager, how would you feel if your colleagues, although of course one had no colleagues to speak of, certainly not when the only reprimands were dealt out to the people with the fewest resources. I wondered now why anyone continued to expend energy, collating evidence, sitting on the carpeted floor of an office, door locked, voices down, only the desk lamp against the five p.m. dark. Truly I marvelled at the men and the destruction they wrought. Just imagine – picture him – this man, this flaccid, round-shouldered, balding fellow in low-tops because of whom so many women would never now be reporters, whose careers had been stopped short. And the people who really could call themselves his colleagues by virtue of their security, their salaries, avowing their allyship on Twitter, saying privately well imagine how difficult it is for him, his marriage falling apart, his mental health, as though only we in the generation below understood that a man could be both sad and a scumbag, that in fact sadness was the excuse these men most often availed themselves of, that and, well, it isn't as though she's particularly vulnerable, the way she holds herself, anyway she's an adult. I was older now, much older, and these days, any disclosures, if and when they came, came unbidden, I turned away from the world, I no longer wanted to hear, one knew after all what happened to those in possession of knowledge unsanctioned by the firm, whatever it was, any small thing that might force a recognition must be suppressed at all costs.

But of course there are disclosures and there are disclosures. A matter of testimony and position, a matter of guilt, of whether one had been compelled by the impoverished morality of the age, the discourses of empowerment, for the edification of the people who stood idly by, or whether it was a matter of bringing into confidence, imposing an expectation of reciprocity that had not been invited in the first place but the refusal of whose terms would nevertheless result in an irrevocable debt or, if accepted, in yet another piece of intelligence used to exact or enact one man's will. In that first car ride from the airport, my brother had made a category error, or perhaps he felt it was I who had not understood the structure of the encounter, had failed to live up to the obligation his confession about the ruin of his marriage entailed. When he returned from his work trip, invigorated, no doubt, by some acquisition or merger, vaguely predatory in nature, that his work had involved him in, he set about reordering the dynamic in the house, the dynamic whose fleeting disarrangement might have been fatal to us both. When he began once more, over the course of that first week, to unspool whatever secrets remained between us, some but not all of which I already knew or surmised, no exegesis was necessary, I understood his purpose. But for my part, no revelation was possible. I had lived simply and alone, had done so little, had been uncompromising. And so, in exchange for my brother's terrible disclosures, I communicated by gesture and expression a sense of being beholden to him, an aspect of fear and awe, not totally manufactured.

For in all honesty I had not known some of what my brother told me, beginning the story as he did in the early decades of another century, right here, in this place, with our ancestors, not all of whom had been innocent victims, no, my brother said, and while not in a position to collaborate per se, nor even to denounce anyone else, our grandfather, our father's father, certainly had an anticipatory view of his own life that did not end in the usual ailments that cropped up in the lore of our people, such as cholera, such as fanaticism, such as the pogroms. In short, our grandfather had high hopes that were to be – that indeed could only be – extinguished in time, in exile, in the new world, with our father. But a man alone cannot make a future. We were begot, and though by choice or incapacity I remember very little of those years inside the family, still I see my mother filleting the carp, saving the bones, saving the head, adding onion, adding carrot, adding oil and sugar, salt and pepper, blending well, cracking the eggs, a spoonful of water, chilling the mixture, returning later to form it into balls. I can picture her even now stuffing the kishke, salting the liver, breading the chicken, chopping the herring.

The story my brother told, very scant on detail, nevertheless explained much about my brother himself, who had always despised weaklings, detested victims, found self-pity, personal grief and collective mourning abhorrent. For a man whose commitment to his own interests was so very serious, it must be, I reflected, no small thing to throw off the yoke of one's history. He had done very well for himself in that regard. He could easily understand the people of the town, he told me one golden summer evening, as we sat looking out on to the garden, their attitudes then, their attitudes now, how they felt they had got a raw deal, had been cut off from fortune by some accident of fate, merely because what at a certain point they and their forebears had called efficiency the rest of the world had, in stages, and one by one, rather like dominoes falling against one another in a tidy sequence until they found themselves all together in a heap, until everything came to an end, determined to be acts of barbarism. And how many of those claiming to be upright had agreed that none was too many? And how many of them in truth, in their heart of hearts, could say they were not guilty? What after all was the difference between thought and deed? Was it a question of scale, or of systematisation? What about the pit parties? What about the dogs? It was no wonder, my brother said, that this bitterness had rever-berated across the generations here: forbidden to speak publicly, directed privately to accept one's responsibility as the criminal party and as a result so many of them had quietly, quietly bided their time. Just think, my brother said, shaking his head, of the terrible spectacle of the post-war years, the public trials, the keening, the memorials. Nothing could have been more monstrous than that. No, my brother said, he could well understand how an antipathy might linger, if he himself had to choose between resentment and self-pity, he would choose the former any day, any day. And the students today, the young people, the women and minorities, supposedly oppressed, were they not committing these very same crimes over again, in their apportionment of blame, the speaking engagements picketed, the publishing contracts cancelled, he said, running his fingers through his hair. Was that not persecution? How, my brother asked, was that any different from the windows smashed, the burning of the books? Such were my brother's views on the unfolding of history, or at least such were the views my brother expounded, as a way of educating me, perhaps, if one were to interpret his claims as a kind of extended allegory in which all my worst qualities might be revealed, if only I would apply myself to its study; or perhaps it was a way of showing me where his loyalties would lie, if push came to shove, if shove came to slaughter, if the rumblings in the town gathered themselves into a more defined shape, perhaps even into an event. All of this is to say that I am sure he felt his speech was a display of his virtuosity, how could I disagree, he spoke so well, yes, and the trees covered the sky a little more each year.

Once he had settled back into the routine of the countryside, my brother, who, as I have said, came from a family of readers, and though he was not a reader himself, valued the didactic function of reading, believed in the novel in particular as a form of directed moral education, took it upon himself to prescribe me a course of daily reading. I had, he said, become slack in my intellectual training while he had been away, so far as he could tell my reading and writing practice had been limited to transcription and, while he granted that copying out had its own pleasures, was in some quarters understood to be a nascent form of translation, the legal profession was not particularly known for its love of language – rhetoric, the art of argumentation, perhaps, indeed, he granted it that, said my brother, shrugging his shoulders, but language, no, it had no feel for it, had no interest in beauty, could not believe in the transformative power of the word. As far as the law was concerned, my brother said, life was set down in the word, but as he saw it, the word, language, could make things possible. Language and its affordances, said my brother, and this time I did not disagree with him. Form and experiment. Meaning ran one way and then another. How lovelily he spoke, I thought again, and to please him, I began to wake early each morning and read a few pages of Montaigne from the copy he had supplied me with. In truth I took almost nothing from these daily readings, though I liked the sound of the author's pronouncements, and I could occasionally be persuaded to issue some or other of his more aphoristic statements at dinner time, to the great and obvious pleasure of my brother. When I stumbled, and I often stumbled, over the phrasing, my brother would slowly and patiently enunciate each word, which I repeated as well as I could. My method of speech had always been unsatisfactory to my brother, as a girl I had been sent to elocution lessons, to a speech therapist, and my brother himself would undertake repetition exercises of the kind I have just described. In spite of all the labours of these various professionals to whom I was presented during my childhood, during my adolescence, I spoke the same as ever, always trailing off into silence.

I had learned much on the subject of silence, about its uses, from my brother, whose expert modulation of speech and silence, the interval between the two which could not quite be called conversation, which I often thought must be a space of transcendence, of mutual annulment, communicated as much if not more of his mood, of his tastes, of his dissatisfaction, than either of the two polarities. My brother knew how to interpret, to impute, to notate, knew in other words how to wield power. As I struggled through Montaigne each morning, I felt the greatness of his intellect, its expansiveness, and, in spite of this, and truth be told, I felt slightly ashamed on his behalf. Was it that I felt, instinctively, that it was improper to use one's mind in public, in so public a way? Was it, in the final analysis, a disgraceful, even obscene thing to think out loud, still worse to have one's thoughts outlive oneself, to travel through the centuries in no straight line, surviving only because of the vagaries of taste, the accidents of translation, to make it through so much only to end up in the hands of some person like me, so ill equipped to receive them? To be acted upon – what was that? One's passivity, one's collusion, the lines only appeared to be clearly drawn. There was something unthinkable in other people, always, I felt that so keenly now, as the green of the leaves kept on quickening, as the light changed, as I saw more clearly that my position vis-à-vis the townspeople was an immovable one, that I had been elected, for purposes whose meaning I still groped for, and for life. Anthropology had not been my area, the social sciences never of particular interest to me, and yet I sensed dimly the outlines of complex networks of exchange and relation that structured the society one lived in, structures that in certain cases required the presence, or more appropriately the exclusion, of a particular individual or object, to enable the cohesion of the whole. One played one's part, everyone did, and it was not that I objected on principle but rather that I could not yet see the whole picture, I did not yet understand my place in the locality outside my brother's home.

My brother's motives in all this were and remain secondary, though I can see how they might be of interest in according him a specific designation, in setting him down as this, as that, for good and all. But I do not claim to speak for anyone – not for my brother, not for the townspeople, least of all for myself. For what could I say? That we grant those close to us an enduring state of exception, that we exempt them from any defiling charge? Perhaps that the events that mark our time on earth move between the unspeakable, the semi-speakable and the simply untoward. Or else and finally that reading is not the equivalent of explanation and while the teller has much to answer for, it is not the meaning itself, no. Communication is a problem, yes, yes, we have already gone through all that. One grows so tired of these demands, these imprudent efforts to set things down once and for all. How did one get here? My brother and his reading lists, Montaigne and of course and never far behind passages of Novalis, Novalis whom he loved above all other thinkers, whose writings he kept close at all times, a paperback copy in his briefcase, the same copy he had trailed around in childhood, he was a strange boy, my brother, one never felt he was destined for success, no, somehow only that he would be a failure, and yet he applied himself, one had to give him that, he had been rigorous, he had been disciplined. He had, ultimately, overcome his circumstances, perhaps even his destiny, yes, that future-orientated word so laden with the past, by observing the rules of order, order and subordination, how little things change, and here I repeat myself, how few the options one's world makes available, how much harm comes again, beginning again and again.

In my brother's house, under my brother's dominion, I found that, perhaps as a result of adhering to the timetables he had created for us, I too came to love orderliness. Where my attentions had been energetic and haphazard they became methodical and restrained. In this way, my brother and I found peace, for a while. The days slowly grew shorter, and I worked to submerge myself once more. Time passed, and I went under. That's all. My brother prevailed, as we always meant him to. In the valley, the townspeople carried on their routines, carried on down their inevitable paths. I continued to present myself at the barn, day after day, my brother took up once again his circuit of visitation, his perambulations taking him from business to business, from door to door. But not all was well. Around the house and grounds, I dealt with a number of small accidents and overlookings. A shattered window, a split tree branch. The bins collected now only intermittently, so that I was required to take the household waste by bicycle to the tip at the farthest edge of town. The tip was presided over by a blond and smiling man who, on my first visit, I found standing on a mattress atop a high mass of rubbish, jumping up and down in an effort to compress it. He spoke no English but managed nevertheless, from the great mound on which he stood, to convey a series of very precise instructions as to where to deposit the various bin bags and sacks of recyclables I had brought with me. He never approached me on any of my visits, though once I saw him peering out from the net curtains of a yellow and white caravan that sat just to the side of the tip's entrance. What was his life like? This young man who spent his days organising the cast-off food and belongings of the township into what seemed to me like a highly sophisticated and complex system. I felt that if this man resented me, it would not be for the same reasons as the rest of the townspeople, it would be for something else, closer to the truth, though perhaps as with so many things the two rationales would inter-sect, at the point of class, at the point of misery. I would wave to him, hello and goodbye, as I came and went, and although he never returned any of these waves, neither did he turn away in disgust.

One morning, well after midsummer, I stepped out to have a furtive smoke while I drank my coffee, for I had to tell the truth taken up smoking once again, and again took up the mantle of shame for being a smoker, a facet of my personality I had always taken pains to hide from my family, though many of my siblings were pack-a-day smokers, or part-time smokers, or social smokers, or at the very least cigar smokers, themselves. I was leaning on the wall on the left side of the door when, looking over, I noticed a strange character carved into the upper third of the right-hand post, within approximately eight centimetres of the doorway opening. I had never before seen this carving, it was not from an alphabet familiar to me, certainly not Latin or Greek; not Cyrillic, Hebrew or Arabic, none of these, no. And it was finely chiselled into the wood frame, someone had evidently taken care in forming this character, had done so with a woodworking tool of some kind, an awl, perhaps, though I could not say for certain. I admired the craftsmanship of it, yes, I knew good work when I saw it, could discern the commitment and even love that had gone into a particular piece of work, though I was impossibly inept myself, clumsy of hand, with slow reflexes and poor peripheral vision. For these reasons I had never learned to drive, and the bicycle I mastered only with great difficulty and after months of effort, practising in secret, in the dead of night, in the empty car parks of malls and other places of business. The appearance of the strange character – a rune? – did not especially faze me, so much had happened in my life in the last few months, and I understood very little of the motions of the universe, the particular streams of energy or movements of fate, that made any of it happen. Neither did I trouble my brother with my concerns, he was busy with work, his work that meant so much to him, but given the nature of the goings-on, related as most of them had been to the maiming, madness or murder of the local animal life, I worried especially for Bert, who, my brother insisted, despite my protests, must be allowed out on his own. My brother did not like to encourage dependence, and he could see that I had developed an attachment to the little dog. This he worked swiftly to correct. Among other actions he undertook to this end, he removed Bert's bed from my room upstairs, and brought it back into the kitchen; he forbade me from sitting in the garden while Bert undertook his daily laps – besides, he pointed out, one could hardly sit outside now that the mosquitoes were out, I must not be ridiculous. As ever, I agreed with my brother, my behaviour had always been ridiculous, if not insane or even criminal, and by and large I acceded to his will. And yet I still watched Bert when I could, concealing myself behind the curtains in order to peer out on to the garden. He seemed untroubled. He seemed the same as ever.

As I cycled across town, to the dump, to the farm, as I cycled back up the hill to my brother's house, I thought often about life and its chance encounters, the inexorable question of complicity, about how not one of us could claim to be innocent any longer. I thought that naivety, though it had long proven useful in protecting one from facing facts more squarely than it suited, was more inexcusable, more repugnant than ever. No more padding between the word and the world. I read once that ours was a century of half measures, and I thought even then that nothing could be further from the truth. Every single one of us on this ruined earth exhibited a perfect obedience to our local forces of gravity, daily choosing the path of least resistance, which while entirely and understandably human was at the same time the most barbaric, the most abominable course of action. So, listen. I am not blameless. I played my part.

Because for all that I did suffer, knowing what crimes were being laid at my door by the townspeople, knowing that they thought badly of me, I knew too that in some sense, so far at least as they were concerned, I had actually done the things I had been accused of. So

I suffered, but I did not allow myself to be consoled, my life's practice had taught me one must not weep that one may not be comforted, and so I pressed on, for my brother, who needed me more than ever. For it seemed to me, or anyway I began to notice, that some barely perceptible change had occurred in his person, in his behaviour. At times, for instance while I bathed my brother in the mornings, while I read aloud to him the headlines of the day's news, I thought I heard him sigh. He was inattentive, no longer asking me to speak up, to enunciate more clearly, to control the vocal fry, to speak from my diaphragm, at times I even found him sitting, eyes glazed, on the edge of his bed. And yet for the most part he continued in his usual routine, he carried on with his work and his telecommuting, holding forth on telephone calls, on Microsoft Teams, I could hear his voice carrying through the oak-panelled door of his study. His meetings with the townspeople carried on, too, his public life unaffected, it seemed, and yet each time I scrubbed his back, each time I executed his Indian head massages, he seemed ever so slightly diminished, the hairline receded by a fraction of a millimetre; a filament of muscle, once taut, slackened, just a little. I did not of course mention any of this to my brother, who had always been so proud of his physique, of his luscious locks, I would do anything to save him the slightest bit of difficulty or discomfort. Nevertheless, I would, I felt, have to take matters into my own hands, in the interests of his health, of his well-being, and I reassured myself with the thought that if he seemed a little paler than usual, a little looser in the flesh or thicker around the middle, all that was needed (and this I reasoned after undertaking some Internet research on the subject) was a vigorous regimen of dry brushing to exfoliate his skin, to unclog his pores, to improve the circulation of his blood, to assist with his digestion, in short to stimulate his nervous system in a variety of ways in the interests of promoting his health. Yes, it was just the thing.

The particular method had suggested itself to me after watching a television programme one evening, on mute, of course, subtitles off, since the latter, my brother had always maintained, made almost as much noise as the sound itself, something in the frequency of the light, he had always been a highly receptive person, my brother, his senses on high alert at all times, his sense of smell in particular, he could not abide odours or perfumes of any kind, was a supertaster into the bargain, and so I learned early on to read the lips of the actors on television, and even when these actors faced away from the camera, still I knew what they were saying. Yes, you will think, after all it is not so hard to follow the plot lines of the insipid television programmes aired hourly and in hysterical profusion on every channel, from every corner of the world, surely it was not so much that I knew what the actors were saying, everyone knew that their voices became quite beside the point, so much could be gleaned from movement and context. Well, I might respond, perhaps. And yet I maintain that it was the dialogue that I followed, the words themselves. However. I will not press the point. Let us move on. Now this programme had been about horses, and I watched as these horses, a sullen and disconsolate lot, not at all biddable, always bowing their heads to eat the grass that grew by the roadside, in the process propelling their riders forward and sometimes clear off their backs, so sudden and forceful were their movements, these same and morose horses were transformed, I mean completely transformed, by a thorough brush down at the hands of the stable team. Where previously their ears remained perpetually pinned back, their hind hoofs cocked, their postures became relaxed, they chewed thoughtfully. My excitement, not to say delight, upon seeing such a turnaround in these horses, of whom everyone had despaired, who had indeed, suggested the host of the show in dark undertones, been but hours away from being sent to the proverbial glue factory, so unpleasant was their disposition, so total their change in manner, was such that I would have risen from the couch and proceeded immediately on my bicycle to the village, to the hardware store, to procure such a brush in aid of my brother's health. But the night intervened, as it so often did, and although the townspeople were capable of much, much too much, keeping their businesses open past regular working hours was beyond them – at least so far as I could see, and I recognise that I had only my eyes with which to do so, and those eyes, it was true, were those of one who was and would remain a stranger. And so I resolved that as soon as business hours resumed, the very next day, I would get on my bicycle and proceed down the road, dressed as it now was in the baked-earth colours of late August, directly, and without stopping, to the hardware store in town.

The streets of the town were eternally empty, except for the dust, which whispered in the still, warm air. It was a dry season. The shop's bell tinkled from the top of the door as I entered. It was like the street, unmanned, and everything covered in a fine layer of dust. I crept around the shop's single room, looking for signs of its keeper, I inspected every corner and checked in every cabinet. I peered over the glass counter, under whose pane and through whose covering of grime I could just see an array of the pastries and sweets for which the town was famous. Behind the counter crouched a man I assumed to be the proprietor, who seemed to be practising some manner of defensive manoeuvre. He looked up at me. Satisfied that my presence had been acknowledged, that I could not be accused of having entered the shop on false pretences, that I was a customer like any other, I walked around the shop perusing the impressively thorough selection of brushes on offer, ranging in size from the infinitesimal – designed, I reasoned, to brush the teeth of a cat – to the immense – this perhaps to smooth the skating rink erected on the town's lake each winter. Somewhere in the middle of these two (for the tools were arranged by size) I found three brushes roughly adequate to the dimensions of my brother, that could provide coverage and relief to his longest flank as well as to his littlest fingers. I brought these to the counter, behind which the shopkeeper was now lying in a recovery position with his eyes closed. I waited. The shopkeeper remained immobile. I coughed. Same result. He looked very peaceful, lying there, the shopkeeper, sleep or coma or perhaps death had smoothed away the signs of age and anger from his face, leaving him with the appearance of a much younger man, a child, even a baby. Yes, after all, there was something decidedly cherubic about the fellow, a quality he had not had while conscious but which he now possessed in spades. After a time, I drew some of the local currency out of the pocket of my jacket and placed it, silently – not wanting to disturb his rest – on the counter. I reached over and beneath the glass top of the counter and removed, too, what, on eating, proved to be an apple strudel. I licked each of my fingers in turn and set off back to my brother's house, pedalling swiftly. I felt strong and purposeful.

My brother did not readily consent to the proposed regimen of dry brushing. I could not understand these objections and at first sought to press my point, something I had never before done. After a stand-off of several days, during which time he did not allow me to draw his bath, read to him, light the fire, cook any meals, do any serving, cleaning or airing out, I reconsidered my approach. My brother, I felt, was trying to communicate something to me in this matter, though I could not be sure of the specifics of his message. I resolved to try to listen to him carefully at the first favourable opportunity, not for the conventional meaning of what his words conveyed, but for the deeper and simpler truth he was no doubt working to express. And so I listened attentively, patiently, to his objections. I listened to them at length, over a series of hours, a series of days, I listened, probing my brother, egging him on, pursuing him along the corridors of his house down which he fled, dogging his steps even to the very door of his office, of his bedroom, of his en-suite bathroom, until at last and quite suddenly he stopped speaking at all. It was at this point, once I had taken the time to listen closely, so very closely, that I found that my brother had always been in agreement with me, of course he was, and what's more, that the whole enterprise had actually been of his own conception. I put this to him, as he sat on the edge of his bed one morning, mute, waiting for me to dress him. Something, some tremor, passed across his face, but he turned away before I could read it clearly. I understood this as assent. And so I presented myself promptly at a time appointed by me to begin the work of my brother's recovery. Sure enough, even after this very first session, I could see my brother rally a little. Yes, I maintain that he rallied after these treatments, a twinkle returning to his eye, a brusqueness to his manner, several hours or even days would pass before he began to slow down once again, to droop his head as he sat at his desk, at which time I would take my brother in hand and execute the therapeutic dry brushing once more. By and by the intervals of high spirits experienced by my brother shortened; sometimes only an hour had passed before

I would notice him dragging his feet as he crossed the hall to his study, at times wearing only slippers or even, and I was to tell the truth quite shocked to see it, in his stockinged feet, and I was required to interrupt his work, his very important work, which he conducted now exclusively over email, in order to minister the now-hourly treatment, which I suspended only for a few hours at night, to allow for a restorative sleep. I began to supplement the dry-brushing sessions with lymphatic drainage massages, a technique I learned from watching instructional videos I found on YouTube, there being no municipal library in the environs, and certainly none that would cover homeopathic remedies of this or any other kind. And so, after I completed his dry-brushing session, I would apply a gentle but increasing pressure to his collarbones, to his underarms, to the insides of his elbows, then subsequently to his legs, with the intention of bringing about, first, the clearing of the lymphatic fluid, and subsequently the absorption of the same. The whole process began on the hour every hour and took anywhere between fifteen and thirty minutes so that I was dedicating fully half of our waking hours – mine and those of my brother – to these remedies. To be sure I felt fulfilled, perhaps for the first time in my life, the very first time, I was giving myself up at last and entirely to my brother body and soul, occupying every corner of him, bending to his will, or in the absence of will, bending at the very least to the needs of his body, the needs of his soul, to have his life be the only duty of another, to be venerated. All his teachings, I felt, through childhood, through adolescence, to this day, had been leading to this point, my sublimation of myself in my brother, for my brother.

If I needed to go into town to shop, or if I presented myself at the community farm to undertake the decreasing number of tasks that had been entrusted to me, of an ever-lower order and which did not involve interacting with animals, potables or edible plants directly, if I needed to leave my brother for any length of time, I knew he would exhaust himself by going into his study to work and that, upon my return, my efforts to keep him on the path to health would have to be redoubled. My brother, such a beautiful speaker, a man who took such obvious and frequent pleasure in holding forth before a crowd, before a small group, before even a lone individual, spoke not at all. I could see however that he was still making a great effort to speak, he would catch my eye, take a moment to steel himself, breathing in through his nose and out through his mouth. He looked so like he had looked in the past, at the height of his powers, as he stood before one on a dais or a stage, about to deliver some life-altering pronouncement, and yet when he finally opened his mouth, a process which in itself took at least five minutes, all that could be discerned was a series of abortive utterances that sounded like he had given up speaking after the first letter, or else as though he were issuing a low groan. This grieved me. What he needed, I knew, was rest, rest at last.

I did my utmost, I tell you, to support him, so that he might, even in his then-developing sickness, continue to inhabit the person of the respected businessman in this northern provincial town, a man at once cosmopolitan and rooted in the countryside, a man who could drink with the local sheriffs just as easily as with the Minister of Energy, a clean and contemporary man. In spite of these efforts, my brother's health continued to decline.

Still I pressed on, without distinction, renouncing even despair, waiting on my brother, cooling his fevers, reviving him from his lethargies, tending to the health of his gut, the dexterity of his limbs, the movement of his vital fluids, the pink of his complexion, the promotion of his salubriousness foremost in my thoughts at all times, yes, I made sure of that. To this day I maintain that I acted in the best interests of my brother, at least as I understood them at the time, an understanding that was, granted, somewhat limited by the problems of communication already outlined and from which I have always suffered, also by the natural reserve of my brother, his will to power, but I did my best. Still his health declined. As time went on, he stopped responding altogether to my physical ministrations. He had reached, it seemed to me, his terminus, a point from which he would neither ameliorate nor deteriorate. He confined himself mostly to his room, padding across the floorboards in his bare feet, looking out each window in turn, looking into the corners, watching his shadow turn on the walls.

Soon autumn came. The season changed at once, clicking over in the night, the air clarified of its balmy undertones, cool and sure. The wind followed shortly thereafter, bringing with it the rain, bringing the particular melancholy of September. I lit the fires, I kept the Rayburn going, I decorated the house in harvest colours. I went for long walks while my brother paced the floorboards. I felt strong and brown and wind-blown.

7

A MEDITATION ON SILENCE

November brought the trouble. A pale month in which I had never especially got on, always preceded by the most glorious October, low sunshine on the blazing trees, days of wind and rain, which I spent gathering the last of the blackberries, stocking the woodpile, hooking and weaving avidly though not at all well. As my brother retreated into his indisposition, he became more vehement about his privacy, keeping his door shut, which he had done so seldom before, having always stipulated that all doors remain open, he especially liked to dress in the doorway of his room, making sure I watched, he liked me, too, to keep open my door, located at such a curious angle that no matter where I stood in the room I could not go unobserved. But now he kept his door shut, and if I kept opening all the doors in the house I cannot be faulted for that, it was a habit so deeply inculcated in me by my brother, after many months of study, yes, I could hardly help myself, nevertheless he found himself in the position of locking the door to his bedroom and to his study, he wanted his privacy, even I could see that, and so I made sure he did not know that I had obtained keys to all the rooms in the house, had even sent away for a skeleton key, I fretted so over my brother's sickness, and I waited until after dark to creep into his room, waited until the middle of the night, when I was sure my brother would be asleep, to watch over him, to make sure he was breathing. I had procured a small hand mirror for just this purpose, to reassure myself that my brother breathed still, he slept so quietly, was so inert, that night after night when I entered his room I feared the worst. As a result of these night-time vigils at my brother's bedside, I found myself less able to work during the day – certainly not at my own job, which required precision and focus. Since the nights came so swiftly, there was less to do around the house, I had been thorough in my handling of the wood-pile, in the collecting, boiling, canning and preserving of various edibles, and found myself free to walk the autumn woods, to walk the barren moor above, from the brief stretch of time from dawn to dusk, crossing the landscape as if I had any right to it, and in my defence the rights-of-way laws that had been implemented twenty years earlier applied even to me, whose citizenship in the place was tenuous, even I would not be accused of trespassing in these places, at least not to my face, per-haps in the private bar, perhaps in the back room of the village shop or the booths of the café attached to it, yes, but I at least never heard it said, and of course even had I heard it, I would not have understood it, thankfully, thankfully. And yet, and unquestionably, I did trespass. My presence violated some crucial and unspoken rule, which I thought now had to do with narrative, the right of a people to preserve the stories they told about them-selves and their own history. My silence was a reproach to them, something pressing at the edges of their con-sciousness, a terrible knowledge they did not want to own and which I made them look at day after day. In silence, yes, for words have more than once led us away from truth.

That year, for the first time, I did not feel my usual dread if I found myself outside in the afternoon as darkness gathered. Instead, I felt myself dissolving into the blue air, as if the atoms that made me up had been loosed and were beginning to disperse, becoming part of the darkness. No one kept me there, and yet nobody had made me leave. And why had they not made me leave? I looked down at my feet, well and warmly shod, and thought, but who can need such boots on these eternally empty paths? What terrain would I have to walk across before whatever was coming arrived, what field, bog or mudflat, what rocky outcrop? The thought surprised me. I looked up and realised I had reached the top of the moor. The sun had slipped behind the mountains that ringed the town. The first stars were twinkling in the darkening sky. And far, far down in the valley, I saw lights on in the church. A grave and pious people, I thought, and felt a shock of cold blow through me. What depths I had left unplumbed, what spirits still to awaken. I heard a stirring sound behind me, the soft footfall of some creature abroad in the night, I thought, turning to look. Far off were two figures, clad in white, glowing against the dusk. I stood still. The wind came across the moor, bringing the smell of leaves, of berries rotting on their stems, and of a hard frost coming on. The two bright shapes had been advancing towards me, it seemed, for an eternity, and remained still a long way off. So here it all was at last. I had come to this place, whence my ancestors had fled, out of what I recognised at last as an unkillable longing for self-annihilation, no more than I felt I deserved and, moreover, what I felt had been meant for me, the wayward child of a people whose only native merit was that they had survived. They had kept on. For ages they had kept on. And here I was, meeting history at last, proof that my deference, anyone's deference, was the surest and swiftest route to one's own eradication. It would be total.

I awaited the figures, tall and upright, a lifetime passed, and when they stood before me at the close, of the day, of it all, a woman and a man clad in white sweat-suits, who were perhaps – though to this day I cannot confirm it with any certainty – the shopkeeper and the man from the dump, I turned around and led them back across the moor, through the woods, down the long road into the valley and at last to the church, whose windows were aflame with many candles, more candles than I had ever seen in one place. I paused at the threshold. For the first and last time I pushed the doors open and passed through them, the man and woman in white following closely behind.

There in all the pews sat the townspeople, all wearing the same white sweatsuit. They looked comfortable. Their faces flickered in the candlelight. Wind blew through the chinks in the window frames. I proceeded to the chancel, where I saw gathered the woman and her dog, and the man from the garage holding what I could only surmise was the trapped ewe's dead lamb, pickling in a specimen jar. I recognised, too, the man I knew had tended the cows, who had so tenderly, so lovingly slaughtered them, out of necessity, of course, of course, and beside him, a man I supposed to be the keeper of the chickens, since he held one, clucking softly, in his arms. Arrayed on a long table before these townspeople was an empty hessian sack and six pink and tiny things, laid up against six more objects that I recognised at once: the reed men I had woven with such care, with such good will, resurrected from their riverside grave. I walked slowly down the church's central aisle, steadily, one step at a time, feeling all four corners of my feet in the manner my yoga teacher in the city had instructed me, keeping my balance, my focus, breathing into my root chakra, I approached the long table, reaching it at last, standing before it at last, looking from the hessian sack to each of the reed men, the talismans, my eyes skipping over the tiny pink things on first go, on second go – finally on my third pass I forced myself to discern the character of the tiny and pink things in the candlelight. I strained my eyes, and I looked. Six piglets, only a few days old, lay still, cradled by the reed men I myself had made, about that at least there was no doubt. I could feel the eyes of the town on me, the collective breath held as I reached a trembling hand out to touch the piglet on the right, the first piglet, as I found myself calling it, to stroke the soft skin, so much like my own in texture, in colour, even in temperature, these piglets had only lived a few days on this earth, on the community farm, had been called away too soon, for although they looked as if they could be sleeping, already their cells were breaking down, shortly to be assisted by insects, taken away in pieces to feed life elsewhere, yes, but no longer in them. So, yes, here it was at last. The piglets, I knew, had been a source of joy and a symbol of hope for the town, still reeling from the loss of the cows, the confinement of the chickens, and so on and so forth, it was the sow's first pregnancy, all previous efforts to get her in pig had come to nothing, she was a moody girl who did not like to be touched, who eschewed the company of the other pigs, all of whom liked to socialise, liked a collective mud bath or a team rootle through the undergrowth, pigs in general being of course extremely social animals, and yet not this sow, no, from the beginning she had exhibited depressive tendencies, had proven disinterested in the boar, a wonderful beast, had, it was claimed, savagely fought off his advances, or so my brother had told me before he descended into silence. For all these reasons the pregnancy of this sow, who had really turned a corner in recent months, was a cause for celebration across the township. But here they lay, her piglets, for hers they must have been, what other sow of age was there in the area, six of them, all dead, their faces untouched but nevertheless slightly peaked, showing evidence of malnutrition, they were so skinny, these tiny piglets whose tiny ribs, I realised upon further inspection, had been crushed, she had lain on them, I thought, all six of the piglets, could not support their demands, their pulling at the teat, which in the end and judging by their size she had refused them, finding herself exhausted, desperate, impregnated against her will, she had taken this course of action which, although extreme, although devastating, nevertheless followed its own logic, was the only possible course of action for the sow to take.

And what had this to do with me? I had seen the sow only once, stopping at the pigs' enclosure one evening after my shift on the farm, merely to look, merely in the

hopes of catching a glimpse of one or more of the piglets, out of curiosity, out of foolishness. I did not think
anyone had seen me. I supposed this ill-considered visit
set off a series of elisions, arising from some vague and
incomplete understanding of religious prohibitions
relating to swine, a confused memory of the libel, yes,
I could easily see how such an association might be
made. And why now? To this, I am relieved to say, I can
provide a more satisfactory answer. The townspeople
could never have felt an affinity for me, still less could
they experience any sense of allegiance, of that there
was never any doubt. But about my brother I had – mis-
takenly, I saw that now – made certain assumptions.
Taking into consideration, which of course I did, our
shared inheritance – genetic, personal, but above all
historical – I felt it would be only natural for him to have
experienced, at some point or other, a certain level of
attachment to me, fatal although it would have undoubtedly proven. You will say: but surely, given everything,
given what you yourself have related in this overlong
account, surely even you could not be so foolish. To
which I can offer no response. Even so. History, as

someone put it, is the resurrection to the very flesh and bone of the story of division, and so while I had never once doubted my brother's judgement, correct and just as it could only be, still I was bewildered to find that he had been attempting, either from the confines of his room or, when he thought I was out, moving into the front hall, where I caught him at it, to contact people in the town, for what reason I could not fathom, though I racked my brains, though I searched my soul, I could see no reason why my brother, who could not speak, might nevertheless wish to communicate with any of the townspeople, not one of whom had visited him since his illness, since his confinement, who had clearly written him off, I reminded him of this as I took the phone from his hand. My brother's actions were puzzling to me since, in the first place, I had days earlier found it necessary to confiscate his mobile phone, a decision I did not take lightly, and taken only in the interests of his health you understand, social media was a poison, was in all likelihood contributing to his overall enervation, I had explained all this to him with the utmost clarity and compassion. In the second place, my brother, of all people, who had rubbed shoulders with the town's elite, who had sat on various boards of commerce, uninvited, to be sure, but who would ever question my beautiful brother, he of all people knew that there were no medical professionals with the competencies required to treat his condition, peculiar as it was, only I, and this only from long acquaintance and daily study, had any idea of its scope and its effects, which I knew would be inevitably written off as psychosomatic by any doctor, should he succeed in reaching one, a doubtful proposition in itself, so broken was the healthcare system in this remote northern country. Did he want to be sectioned and carted off to the psychiatric ward, I asked him, that perfectly unsuitable lakeside institution with an open-door policy, where the lunatics roamed freely, where he would find himself on the other side of a ping-pong table from some convalescent psychotic who had only recently stopped seeing silverfish all over his skin? Of course not, I said, draping a blanket over his shoulders. The number my brother had been trying to contact – by text message, surely, given his present tendency to muteness – belonged to a certain Herrenhof, a man who claimed to be a medical doctor but whose credentials were doubtful, who worked primarily as it happened in the town's morgue, performing autopsies on all the corpses of the wider county of which this township was the centre. What, I said to my brother, taking him by the shoulders, dead already! Ha! I led him to the sofa in the front room, still chuckling, and at my direction he sat down, so docile his mien, so panicked his eye. I tucked the blanket around him. No, I thought, they would not come for him, he must understand that now, must understand, yes, that history for them was indeed a matter of flesh and bone, that no amount of rehabilitation could make it otherwise; no, those paths had been laid out long ago. One's orientation to the world was a fixed point from which one made one's observations, this at any rate was what the townspeople felt, had always felt, about my brother, even before my arrival: one man could be managed, but any more, any different, and the landscape began to change. One dipped into the valley. It was not that one was contemptible, not necessarily, but rather that one's presence wrung out a deeper sense of abjection, so much more primal than the disgust I usually aroused. Here, one was forced back into one's context, given a kind of depth, no longer an atomised individual but part of a structure of feeling that was centuries old. How capacious it was in comparison! How inevitable! How beautiful to be conscious of the inexorable process of eternal recurrence. I felt held. I hoped my brother would someday feel held by it, too.

Such were my thoughts as I stood contemplating the piglets, regarding their injuries, and regarding the pain of the townspeople, those standing in silence beside the table and those ranged in the pews behind my back, I felt it, the howl of their anger, concentrating itself, not needing any longer to search for an object, having found it at last. I bowed my head before the piglets for the last time, gathered together my will and pressed my body into motion, with difficulty, directing one foot forward and then the other, until I stood behind the dais. I looked out on the assembly.

Allow me to begin by suggesting that there is nothing to say and nothing with which to say it. Whatever has been spoken heretofore, under duress, against one's better judgement, through weakness of will and debility of mind, never stirring from the field of the possible, circumscribing instead a mean little reality, the protection of the frontier, what, I ask, has all that been in service of? The less we are offered, the finer the quality of attention we bring to bear. Do I suggest that a reorganisation of the sensible is possible, of the commonsensible? Not at all, no. I allow myself no horizon of possibility. Where one might expect two poles to meet – at the greatest extreme of enfeeblement – what one finds is only distance and misunderstanding. But I see I have once again committed my usual error, I have

185

forgotten myself once more, overlooking the fact of my own impoverished language, incapable of any image whatsoever, any expression whatsoever. One comes up short, of course one does, short of oneself, short of the world. And yet I see it would not be enough for me to go away, to leave this place, I am implicated personally now where before I had only been implicated historically, yes, it is much too late, I have read the theorists on this point, that things are such that they remain at the boundaries of verbal articulation. The fundamental question that I pose now, that has been posed before and elsewhere, more or less word for word, here it is, my brother, prepare yourself, is whether one can go on living after all, whether one who escaped by accident, one who by rights should have been killed, may go on living. One asks it of oneself, this question posed by all the faces seated before me in the town church, the question that reverberated through the cavernous suburban homes, that was transmitted in the lullabies. What right, what reason did they have, one's ancestors, to flee into the forest, cross the water, peddle rags, go to school – what was it all for, when in the final analysis one was never meant to survive? What was left? And was it enough to carry on? But we begin to weary of this line, do we not? Because here, after all, we are.

After standing on the dais for a time, I stepped down. The faces of the townspeople remained unreadable to me, unreadable as their language, as their law, as the land itself. Not everything was possible, I reminded myself. So much was refused in advance. So much transpired on a scale of time and space that was longer than a lifetime, wider than a country, vaster than the story of the exile of a single people. And bigger still.

These days my brother pads from room to room in his bare feet, in silence. His hair grows long. I cook and clean for him, I groom him and read to him. Bert dozes by the fireside. Outside, night gathers around the house. I breathe in and out, this uncanny air. Today, as I write, it is the winter solstice. The land sleeps beneath the snow, the boughs of the pine trees dip down under its weight. In the coming days the townspeople will celebrate their holiday in the church, whose lights I can see even now from the window where I stand. Beyond my brother's garden, far away down in the valley. I know they will not come because they do not need to.

Nevertheless, I say to myself, softly, I am living, I claim my right to live.

References

pages 27–8   Woolf, Virginia. *The Diary of Virginia
                Woolf, Volume 1 1915–1919*, 1977. The
                Hogarth Press; Malone, Patricia.

pages 29–30   Fitzgerald, Penelope. *Offshore*, 1979.
                HarperCollins; de Montaigne, Michel.
                The Complete Essays, trans. M.A. Screech,
                2004. Penguin.

page 34   Sontag, Susan. *As Consciousness Is
                Harnessed to Flesh: Journals and Notebooks,
                1964–1980*, 2012. Penguin.

page 53   Weil, Simone. *Gravity and Grace*, trans.
                Emma Crawford and Mario von der Ruhr,
                2002. Routledge.

page 85   NDiaye, Marie. *Ladivine*, trans. Jordan
                 Stump, 2017. MacLehose.

page 96   Whitman, Walt. 'Song of Myself', *Leaves of
                 Grass*, 2008. Oxford World's Classics.

page 111   de Montaigne, Michel. *Complete Essays*.

page 134   Riding, Laura. *Experts Are Puzzled*, 2018.
                 Ugly Duckling Presse.

page 139   Clifton, Lucille. 'robert', *The Collected
                 Poems of Lucille Clifton, 1965–2010*, 2012.
                 BOA Editions; Charman, Helen. 'They
                 Shoot Horses, Don't They?', *Academics
                 Against Networking #1*, 2019. Nell Osborne
                 and Hilary White.

page 144   Malone, Patricia.

page 174   Alexievich, Svetlana. *The Unwomanly Face
                 of War*, trans. Richard Pevear and Larissa
                 Volokhonsky, 2018. Penguin; Kafka, Franz.
                 The Castle, trans. J.A. Underwood, 2019.
                 Penguin; NDiaye, Marie. *That Time of Year*,
                 trans. Jordan Stump, 2020. Two Lines Press.

pages 180–1   Minh-ha, Trinh T. 'White Spring', *The
                 Dream of the Audience, Theresa Hak Kyung
                 Cha (1951–1982)*, ed. Constance M.
                 Lewallen, 2001. University of California
                 Press.

page 185   Beckett, Samuel. *Proust and Three Dialogues with Georges Duthuit*, 1965. John Calder.

page 107   Bachmann, Ingeborg. *Malina*, trans. Philip Boehm, 2019. Penguin.

Acknowledgements

Thanks as ever to Harriet Moore at DHA, and to Jason Arthur and Josie Mitchell at Granta, for supporting the writing of this book.

Special thanks to Gerry Irvine, who told me a story about a ewe caught in a fence, and to both Gerry and Mark Irvine for letting me borrow the name of their noble dog, Bert.

To my beloved friends, who teach me so much about collaboration and care, writing and life, Yanbing Er, Claire Gullander-Drolet, Patricia Malone, Alison

MacLeod, Chantelle Rideout, Mike Saunders, Hilary White, Lizzie Wilder Williams, Richard Williams, Rosie and Xoo Williams: thank you and sorry for everything.

To my beloved family, whom I can never hope to properly thank or apologise to: Nat Bernstein, who is so missed, Janice Woodfine, who keeps us together, to Jesse Bernstein, Hugo Popovic Bernstein, Shelan Markus: I'll try – thank you.

And to Robin Irvine, for our wretched, muddy and good life.